The Wright Twist

by Josie Daval

ORANGE FRAZER PRESS
Wilmington, Ohio

ISBN 1-933197-19-6

Additional copies of *The Wright Twist* may be ordered directly from:

Orange Frazer Press
Wilmington, OH 45177
937.382.3196
www.orangefrazer.com

Chapter illustrations by Margaret Hawley Morgan
Cover illustration by Andrea Levy
Design and layout by Chad DeBoard

Library of Congress Cataloging-in-Publication Data

Daval, Josie, 1961-
  The Wright Twist / by Josie Daval.
     p. cm.
Summary: Leah, a twelve-year-old Ohio tomboy and middle child in a family inclined to practical jokes and experiments gone awry, spends the summer of 1905 in adventures with her older brothers, including sneaking a peek at the crazy Wright men and their new flying machine.
  ISBN 1-933197-19-6
[1. Family life--Fiction. 2. Wright, Orville, 1871-1948--Fiction. 3. Wright, Wilbur, 1867-1912--Fiction. 4. Airplanes--Fiction.] I. Title.
  PZ7 D2715Wri 2006
  [Fic]--dc22   2006048305

DEDICATION

To my Father Who has loved me forever,
and my family who love me day by day.

I am truly blessed!

ACKNOWLEDGEMENTS

So many people have helped me with this endeavor that to thank each one would be a book in itself. My husband has been vital—he encouraged me to chase a dream and gave timely pep talks when my dreams were taking a lot more work than expected. My daughter has been my chief sounding board and was the one to tell me, "No, you cannot write a nonfiction account; this needs to be fiction!" I listened and here we are. My son also added his two cents and kept me well supplied with needed hugs.

The Montgomery County Historical Society offered great direction as I began to dig into Dayton's history. Jeff Opt was extremely helpful with the NCR information. The Dayton Public library didn't ban me from coming back, even when I checked out way too many books or stayed in their local history room for long stretches. The rangers at the various Historical locations—Huffman Prairie, the Third Street bike shop, and Carillon Park—were always glad to answer questions, even when I asked more than my share. To all of you, thanks.

Laura was there to cheer me on and edit my first draft. Mrs. Wolfe let me use her fifth-grade class as guinea pigs and bloodied my second draft. Liz helped me with the final touches. Thank you, dear English ninjas!

Several books were vital in my research: Dr. Tom

Crouch is the Grand Master of Wright brothers knowledge. His book, *The Bishop's Boys: A life of Wilbur and Orville Wright,* is packed with information. In fact, everywhere I looked for information about the Wright brothers, I found Dr. Crouch noted. *Ohio Town* by Helen Hooven Santmyer; *Grand Eccentrics: Turning the Century: Dayton and the Inventing of America* by Mark Bernstein; *The Wright Brothers Legacy: Orville and Wilbur Wright and Their Aeroplanes* by Walt Burton and Owen Findsen; and *Boss Ket; A Life of Charles F. Kettering* by Rosamond McPherson Young were also treasure troves of information. Although the authors don't know it, I couldn't have done this without them. Thank you. I share your love for these amazing men.

My humblest of thanks has to go to God, who promised me, "I can do."

NOTE FROM JOSIE

In *The Wright Twist,* Lee and the gang have the unique pleasure of rubbing shoulders with some very special people. Whenever I read a historical novel I spend a great deal of mental effort wondering which part of the story is real and which is fictional. I have always thought it would be great if someone put a little section in the back of a book that mapped out the real and the not so real—so I did! Now, for those of you who share in my overly active curiosity, there's a glossary in the back where you can check what's real and what's...well, Twisted!

CHAPTER ONE

I was perched in my favorite tree, a giant oak with thick branches that were perfect for sitting. The oak offered an excellent view of the farm. It sat next to my home, just in front of the summer kitchen where my mother was presently cooking. From where I sat I wouldn't miss anything, but I was too far away to get sucked into guilt by association. Not being involved was a good idea, for at twelve years of age I had plans that included living a long and full life. At least I wanted to make it through the summer, and the summer was just getting started.

Straight across from my elevated position sat a big red barn. From my vantage point I could see the front of the building with its giant, double doors wide open, revealing farm tools and equipment neatly arranged in the tidy interior. Above the doors was another smaller door. My fifteen-year-old brother, Lin, stood in the small door, looking out. His brow

1

was furrowed, and he had the look of a man on a mission. He was running one of his experiments with Jasper playing the part of guinea pig. I had tried to get Lin to use the cat, and I almost had him convinced, too. Then Will jumped in. Will, at fourteen, was another older brother—but only by chronology, not by wisdom. At least I didn't think so. Will had a tendency to take things to dangerous levels. After Will convinced Lin to ditch the cat idea and use Jasper, I headed for the tree.

Jasper, otherwise known as "the victim," was standing below Lin, looking up with a detached interest at the activity above. His detachment only reflected his woeful unawareness of the lurking dangers. Once Lin successfully threaded the pulley with the rope he was wielding, Jasper would become the center of activity. Lin fancied himself a scientist and inventor. He seldom passed up a good idea, even when the idea was a bit on the crazy side, like this one. It was Will's idea, and that should have said it all. Will, or Willard as our mother calls him when he's in trouble, had a knack for mischief. Today was a prime example; by using Jasper as the weight, Lin and Will—and poor Jasper, as well—were about to discover the secrets of the pulley.

They had lured Jasper into helping out by offering penny candy, and for a six-year-old candy was everything. Jasper was the baby of the family. Most of the time he didn't seem to have much going on in his head, but then when we least expected it, he'd outsmart all of us. Now that Will and Lin had a willing Jasper, they didn't have to go trap a cat. On our farm trapping a cat was a difficult task. Most of the barn cats had participated in at least one of Lin's experiments and now ran at the sight of him. Even our dog Beans headed under the porch any time he saw Will and Lin together. So they had Jasper, and I was up a tree.

Poor Jasper, he was just a little thing, six years old and scrawny. His face was round and surrounded by hair that went in every direction. His eyes were a brilliant blue, and he would be considered quite cute except that his nose ran—constantly. He had a perpetual streak on his right sleeve from periodic swipes at his leaky appendage. Now, as he watched his brothers, I wondered if he had any clue about what was coming.

Lin recently became obsessed with pulleys. He talked about pulleys, and ropes, and drag, and percentages till we were all sick to death. Will probably suggested this whole mess just to shut Lin up. Today it was time for Lin to finally test his theories. But first Lin had to thread the pulley. It wasn't an easy task since the pulley hung from the end of a beam. The beam extended a good two feet out from the barn above a small door that was located a considerable distance from the ground. Lin's attempts made the whole process look like a circus act. I stopped worrying about Jasper. Lin was much more likely to die merely from his attempt to thread the pulley. He'd probably never get to Jasper.

But Lin finally succeeded at threading the rope and came down through the barn and out the big doors. He talked with Will a moment, then disappeared back inside. A few minutes later he came out dragging a long ladder. The two older boys set it up along the side of the barn right beside the small window. I couldn't help but think, *Too bad he hadn't set the ladder up before tackling the pulley. It would have been easier.* Then just before I said something, I reminded myself that I didn't want to be a part of this mess.

Once they had the two ends of the rope from the pulley on the ground, they attached one end to Jasper by wrapping it around his waist. Then they secured it with a massive knot. After Jasper was all set, Lin fussed over a burlap sack filled with dirt. He added dirt and then dumped some out, working till he thought it was about the same weight as Jasper.

The sack was then tied to the other end of the rope. Lin shouldered the sack and began to labor up the ladder. I thought, *This is so wrong; can they really be doing what I think they're doing?* Sure enough, they were. High up the ladder, Lin called, "Ready Jasper? Ready Will?"

Will checked Jasper's rope one more time, then yelled up, "Let her go!"

Lin let the sack drop. It landed with a resounding thud. Jasper just stood there, watching. I was trying so hard not to laugh I almost fell out of the tree. Finally, I yelled, "Gotta make the rope shorter, boys!" That earned me a glare.

After a minute of consideration, Lin tried to bring the sack up the ladder. Ten feet up, he balanced the sack while trying to tie the rope around it. To Lin's credit, it was more than a minute before he finally lost hold of the bag. And to Will's credit, he could move fast when a bag full of dirt was coming down at his head.

Lin finally lugged the bag inside the barn. A short time later, he and the bag appeared in the upper window. From there he snagged the rope and tied it to the bag. They went through the launching procedure again, and with the "Let her go!" the bag was dropped, and my younger brother was snatched off his feet. He and the bag swung side by side a good six or seven feet up in the air. Although the bag was doing its best to attack Jasper, he didn't seem too concerned. He swiped his nose from time to time and dangled contentedly. I wondered what was going through his mind. He could be thinking, "I should have held out for more candy," or "Hey, look, a sack!" With Jasper, I never knew.

Getting Jasper down was another problem the boys hadn't anticipated. They ended up grabbing him by the leg and pulling him over to the ladder.

Once there, Jasper climbed up the ladder and into the upper window where Will untied him.

All three boys met in front of the barn. Lin and Will, having conducted an experiment of resounding success, were quite pleased with themselves. Jasper was smiling, too, most likely glad to be finished with them. But as the two older boys continued to talk, Jasper's smile faded. A look of panic slowly replaced his smile as Lin and Will started to point and nod.

My heart sank, and I thought, *Oh beans, they are going to go on to round two. Jasper is going to die after all.*

Lin disappeared into the barn. A few minutes later he returned, armed with a variety of pulleys and more rope. He dropped it all in a heap and rummaged through the pile until he found the perfect pulley. Then he and Will searched around the base of the barn and looked for some way to attach the pulley. At one point Jasper started to bolt, but Lin caught him before he could get up any speed. With a threat of physical discomfort and the promise of candy (he was now up to three pieces), Jasper finally agreed to stay put.

Will brought Jasper up to the second floor window while Lin figured out how to work the pulley system. Jasper sat in the window with his legs dangling over the side, swiping his nose, for the next half hour while Will and Lin fiddled. Running the rope from the ground pulley to Jasper wouldn't work.

You know, gravity and all. But then the same problem held true for the sack. The ground just kept getting in the way.

Eventually, Will noticed an eyehook at the base of the window big enough to run the rope through. Since the door acted as an entrance for loading hay in the fall, it had a ramp that ran from the window to the back of the loft, deep inside the barn. He and Lin figured that if they placed Jasper on the ramp they could attach the rope to him. Then they would run the rope from Jasper through the eyehook at the base of the second-story window.

Their thinking was that the eyehook would stop Jasper from following the rope down to the ground since Jasper was too big to go through the eyehook. From the eyehook, the rope ran down the outside of the barn, through the bottom pulley, and then back up through the top pulley. Finally, the rope came back into the second-floor window, where it would be ultimately attached to the weighted sack. The boys' evil plan was coming together.

Will finally came down and grabbed the dirt-filled sack. He lugged it inside the barn and soon appeared at the upper window. He and Lin started debating over the sack's weight. They decided to leave the sack the same weight as Jasper, since they weren't sure if the whole thing would work. They figured their system needed all the help it could get.

Inside, I found out later, Lin put Jasper on the

ramp, away from the window. Once again the rope was tied tightly around Jasper's waist. Will stationed himself outside the barn. Lin readied the sack filled with dirt. He took a spot far to the side of the second-floor window. He looked inside and asked Jasper if he was ready. I can't imagine that Jasper said "Yes," but Lin was satisfied with whatever answer he received. Then he looked at Will. For a brief moment I thought about screaming at the top of my lungs, "No!" Before I could, Lin dropped the sack out of the window. It crashed to the ground.

For a moment nothing seemed to happen—then everything burst into motion. The sack carried more punch than they had expected. Since Jasper had been set so far back on the ramp, he would never have reached the eyehook if the sack had dropped slowly. There was too much rope. Instead, Jasper got to moving so fast that momentum took him the rest of the way up the ramp and out the window. The heavy sack catapulted Jasper out of the window as if he'd been shot out of a cannon.

I squeezed my eyes shut. But Jasper's screams still rang in my ears. All I could think was, "Why didn't I stop them? I could have saved him." Then I was aware that Jasper still hadn't stopped scream-ing. I opened my eyes to see him held firmly by the rope, swinging wildly back and forth through the big double doors, his arms and legs flailing in all direc-tions. The eyehook hadn't stopped him from vacating the barn, but it did stop him from getting dashed to bits on the ground. Will shuffled below him, frantically trying to get him to shut up.

Before we all could get our breath back, we heard the one sound that could freeze the blood in our veins—our mother.

"Lindley David Twist, what's going on out there?"

Already halfway down the ladder, Lin scrambled the rest of the way and ran toward the summer kitchen.

"Nothing, Mama," he yelled, skidding to a stop at the kitchen's door. Just then my mother stepped out.

"What was that sound I heard?" She asked, glancing towards the barn. But Lin had placed himself between her and the excitement. Although only fifteen, he was almost as big as my father. Helping out with the farming had seemed to stimulate his growth.

My mother's name was Rose, or "Rosie" as my father called her. She was about five feet four inches tall with shiny brown hair and blue eyes that sparkled. My mother was quick to laugh with us kids, but we could never pull anything over on her. She was not one to toy with. Now she began to cross-examine Lin.

Behind Lin, Jasper still swung in the barn doorway. Judging by the frequency and energy of his nose-wiping, he was not amused by his adventure. Will was doing his best to keep Jasper quiet.

"Shhhh," Will urgently but quietly pleaded. Jasper was now in a unique position of power. He mouthed to Will, "Seven pieces."

Seven pieces of candy for his silence—ruthless! Will shook his head in horror. Jasper narrowed his eyes and cleared his throat. Will desperately held up four fingers. Jasper mouthed five. Finally, Will nodded. Jasper smiled. And I thought the boy was helpless.

As shaken as he was, Will was having a heck of a time getting Jasper down. With the new pulley setup, Jasper was suspended higher up in the air. Will couldn't reach his foot to pull him to the ladder, and the ladder was too heavy for Will to move alone. He couldn't just untie the sack because Jasper would fall too far. He finally began trying to climb the ladder with the sack. Since he was already flustered—more so because he had just lost so much candy—he wasn't making good progress.

Meanwhile, Lin and my mother finished their talk, and she turned to go inside. Lin turned around and flashed a big grin as if to say, "Boy, did we pull *that* off."

As the door was about to close behind her, my mother called out, "Jasper, once they get you down, come in here. You can help Annie and me with this pie. And Lee—get out of that tree. You're going to rip your dress!" There was just no getting by my mother. She had known all along.

As the door slammed shut, the boys sprang into action. Lin held the rope while Will untied it from the sack. Then Lin slowly lowered Jasper to the ground. As soon as Jasper had both feet on the ground he turned to Lin and said, "I'll tell her it was my idea if you give me seven pieces of candy."

Will and Lin looked at each other. They knew they'd been beaten. Both reached into their pockets and pulled out their precious candy. Three from Lin, three from Will, and the last piece finally squeezed out of Lin, since it was his experiment to start with. "I should have listened to Lee and gone with the cat," he said. "It would have cost less."

There are times when life carries great satisfaction. As I sat in the tree, I let those few glorious words play over and over in my head. "I should have listened to Lee . . . ."

It was a good day.

As soon as Jasper scooted into the kitchen, I heard my mother ask, "So, how much candy did you get?"

As I began to climb out of the tree all I could think was, *Dang, she is good.*

CHAPTER TWO

Apple pie. I knew what *that* meant—Gypsies! Not the Gypsies in the stories that steal horses and kidnap babies. Around Dayton there were a number of wonderful families who were Gypsies. They owned several acres of land. In the summer they'd rent out their fields to local farmers and travel around. Every once in a while they'd come to my family's farm selling all kinds of things. Two of them, Mr. and Mrs. Stanley, had an uncanny knack for showing up anytime my mother made apple pie. Her apple pie was the best in the county. Eventually, whenever my mother made apple pie, we expected visitors. The pies were out of the oven, so I figured they'd be coming any minute.

With that in mind, I scooted down the tree. But scooting didn't work so well in a dress. In my rush, the back of the skirt got caught up on an old branch. When I jumped down the final six feet, instead of landing I ended up suspended a good foot off the ground, with my dress caught up around my armpits. Did I mention I hated dresses? I was stuck good, too. My back was to the tree, so I didn't have any way to get to it. So far no one had noticed the spot I was in, and that was fine. Help would come at a high cost.

Hanging there, I started working on a solution to my predicament all by myself. Then I heard a sound that quickly changed my mind. Bells. The Gypsies' horses wore bells. Shucks! "Lin, get over here, I need your help—quick!"

Lin looked over at me and then turned to Will, "Hey, Will, look at Lee!" Both of them started laughing.

Imbeciles, I thought. "Get over here and help me down."

"Why should we?" Will asked.

"Because if you don't, I'll tell mom what really happened to the dog's tail."

The laughing stopped. The two boys headed over to unhook me from the demon tree. To get me down, Lin had to climb up into the tree and unhook my dress. I had almost made it down before the Gypsies rounded the corner. When it comes to humliation, unfortunately, *almost* doesn't count. At least they had the good grace not to laugh like the boys did. They just pulled up their wagon and stared—even their horses seemed to stare.

They both flashed me a kind smile, but I had to do the only thing proper in such a situation: I ignored everyone. Once free, I dropped to the ground and stomped into the house.

Lin poked his head in the summer kitchen to let my mother know we had visitors. The Stanleys drove their wagon into the courtyard between the house and the barn. By the time I got up to my room and looked out the window, my mother was welcoming them. She greeted the Gypsies as she greeted every-one—like old friends. After a few minutes, they headed to the house. Lin and Will ran into the sum-mer kitchen. Each boy emerged with a pie and fol-lowed the others into the house.

There were times when hard decisions needed to be made. Stay upstairs and sulk, or go face my shame and eat pie...*humm*. My mother's apple pie was one of the great things in life. If I didn't make an appearance, I'd miss out. Easy decision. Besides, the Gypsies were always good for telling the latest goings-on around the area.

I headed to the kitchen and acted like nothing had happened. Although I got a knowing smile from Mr. Stanley, he didn't say anything. Everyone was enjoying pie, and I helped myself to a thick slice. It was still hot from the oven. Then I went and sat on a stool in the corner of the kitchen where I could watch and hear everything.

I loved to watch the Gypsies; they were so myste-rious and unique. Both had hazel eyes, flecked with gold. Mr. Stanley was tall and lean. He had dark straight hair and dark eyes. His skin was deep brown and a big mustache covered his mouth. I could always tell when he was smiling because his eyes danced and his teeth flashed. His wife was equally dark, and her brown hair was wavy and long. Her skirts were flowing and colorful. She wore a bunch of jewelry—several necklaces and hoop earrings and so many bracelets that she jangled when she moved. She was also quick to smile. I thought she was beautiful.

With a start, I realized that I was being studied as well. Mrs. Stanley had been watching me. She leaned over and whispered something in her husband's ear. He threw back his head and laughed. Then he looked at me and winked. I wasn't sure whether to run or just ignore the whole thing. I decided to ignore the whole thing. Running off would only mean I'd miss out on all the excitement.

My mother and the Gypsies began discussing the latest happenings around the area. Who had a baby, who was ill, who was getting married and such. The Stanleys caught her up on all the local events. At one point they said something that caught my attention. They mentioned two brothers, and said with a laugh, "Like your daughter, they fly through the air."

I figured I'd let that pass. He went on to say that the brothers worked a few miles east of our farm, and then he was off to other news. I didn't listen to much else. I was thinking about the brothers. Mr. Stanley didn't say they were *trying* to fly. He said they *were* flying. But then he said I was, too. Oh well.

Before long, it was time for the Gypsies to continue

on their rounds. We all trailed along behind them as they walked out to their wagon. When we got there, Mr. Stanley reached into his pocket and pulled out a piece of gum for Jasper, then rumpled his hair. Jasper smiled, then swiped his nose.

Jasper was the only one they ever gave gum to, and they gave him gum every time they visited. Lin, Will, and I had asked Jasper about it several times, but he'd just shake his head and smile. He loved that it bugged us, and the more irritated we got the more he'd grin. He wouldn't even talk after we tied him up by his feet and left him to hang upside down till his face turned red. Well, we had to *try*.

Then Mr. Stanley reached into their wagon and brought out a huge shiny metal bowl and handed it to my mother. For months she had been saving her egg money for a "biscuit bowl." She practically hugged it. He reached back into the wagon again and Mrs. Stanley handed him something I couldn't see. They smiled at each other and he turned to me. "Leah, we have something very special for you."

My eyes almost popped out and I gasped, "Me? What is it?"

He held out a grey ball of fur. With both hands I took it from him and looked at an impossibly small, grey kitten. The kitten looked up at me and yawned. "He is not an ordinary kitten, my friend, he is very special. You take good care of him. Then, one day you will know it is time for him to move on."

"Move on?" I cried, "No, I'll keep him forever."

Then I came to my senses a bit and turned to my mother, "That is, if I can keep him—Mom?"

She looked at all of us, still clutching her bowl and smiling, and said, "Oh, I suppose so, it's just a little kitten, but you'll have to take care of him."

Mr. Stanley climbed into the wagon and sat down beside his wife. He looked at me and said, "You'll know when it's time for him to move on."

He turned his team around and the wagon started back down our lane. As they pulled away, I heard the both of them laughing.

I shivered and thought, *Okay, that was strange.* But the kitten was amazing. I sat down on the front porch steps with my little sister Annie beside me. The kitty curled up on my lap and began purring. Soon he was fast asleep.

The summer was off to a great start—new and bursting with promises of long days of adventure. Sure, we all had our chores around the farm. Lin helped my father out with the farming; Will helped keep the kitchen stocked with firewood and fed the livestock. My jobs were dusting around the house, washing the dishes, and feeding table scraps to our pig, Pork. Annie helped with the cooking and washing. Cooking should have been my job, but I had no mind for it. Anytime my mother tried to drag me into the kitchen, the results were less than the best. She didn't seem to mind too much and eventually set her sights on my very willing little sister.

I looked at Annie. At age nine, she was everything I was not—cute and tidy. Her eyes were sky blue and her blonde hair fell in soft, perfect curls. Her clothes were always just so. She cuddled her baby dolls, made doilies, and was a great cook. She was so perfect you'd think she'd be irritating, but along with everything else, Annie was a good soul.

Me? At twelve, I'd rather play with my brothers and their friends than stay inside. I could run and jump and spit with the best of them. I was on the tall side and kinda gangly. My straight brown hair was well above my shoulders (due to an experiment gone bad), and my eyes were green. Lin and Will treated me like one of the boys, and I liked that. Lots of times they'd keep me along because I was willing to try most anything.

CHAPTER THREE

That evening while my entire family was at the dinner table, Will gave us quite a surprise. He had been quiet all through the food passing, and Will was never quiet. That should have clued us something was up, but we were all too busy catching up on the day. My father, at the head of the table, was just in the middle of an update on the cornfield when Will piped in, "I was thinking about getting a job."

That brought the dinner conversation to a halt. Everyone looked at him open-mouthed. Finally, my mother said, "Gee, Will, that's a new concept. Where'd it come from?"

"You remember Joe King? His father got him a job over at National Cash Register, and he says they need more workers. I thought it'd be neat to work at the factory. Joe's father is always talking about how nice the factory is. It has big windows, and everyone gets malted milk in the morning..."

"I knew food had to be involved," my father

19

chuckled. "Where would you be working; do you know yet?"

"I'm not sure, but I think I can get a spot as a runner, like Joe. Since I'm only fourteen I can't work on any of the big machines. But being a runner is great. I'd get to go all over the whole place."

"That sounds perfect for you. I don't think they'd be able to keep you in one spot." My father paused, and then said, "Go ahead and apply, and then let us know how it goes."

Will sat back in his chair with a huge grin plastered upon his face.

Then my father looked at me, "I heard you got a gift today."

This was good. I'd been nervous that once my father caught wind of the kitten he might say no. This didn't sound like no. My father, Leo Twist, was a big man, more than six feet tall. So he towered over my mother. His hair was curly and brown, with blond highlights from the sun. His skin was tanned from working outside and his eyes were sea green. He was honest, kind, and patient.

"Mr. and Mrs. Stanley gave me a kitten."

"A kitten? Where is he?"

"Upstairs in a box. Want to see him?"

"Finish your supper first."

I set about stuffing as much food as possible into my mouth at a time. My father looked at me with wonder. My mother laughed and said to him, "It's your fault."

With the last mouthful still puffing out my cheeks, I signaled to leave the table. My mother nodded and I was up the stairs. When I got to the kitten's box, he wasn't there. I quickly looked around my room but couldn't see him. I sat down on my bed trying to figure out what to do next. I could hear my heart pounding in my chest and I tried to settle myself down, but all I could think was, *I lost him.*

Then I heard a quiet scratching. I held my breath. There again, off to my left. I looked over and saw nothing. I got up and looked around the area. Finally I looked inside my dollhouse. My dollhouse sat unused on a tall table in my room. My mother and father gave it to me before they realized I wasn't Annie. Stuffed into one of the tiny rooms with his tail and behind hanging out a window was the kitten.

I tried gently to pull him out, but he seemed to want to stay where he was. I finally ended up winning a tug-of-war with him and looked him over. He didn't seem worse for the wear. He just looked at me like, "What'd you do that for?"

The boys, it must have been the boys. They never quit. The kitten could have climbed out of the box, maybe. But I couldn't imagine him climbing up the table and stuffing himself into the dollhouse. I stomped down the stairs and into the dining room with the kitten in my arms. My father smiled and reached out to take the kitten, but I was mad and paid no mind. "Someone stuffed my kitten into the dollhouse." Once again, silence reigned at the table. Jasper swiped at his nose. My father's smile faded.

"What?" he asked.

"The kitten, when I went up to get him, he wasn't in his box. He was in my dollhouse, stuffed inside like a cork."

My father looked at me and then around the table. "Let's not jump to conclusions, Lee. Did you boys do this?" Lin, Will, and Jasper shook their heads. No. Even Annie shook her head, although everyone knew she'd never do anything of the sort. With another look around the table my father asked, "Are you sure?"

Again, the boys shook their heads.

As we talked it over, we realized that no one was around at the right time to perform the kitten-stuffing. The boys were innocent after all.

After I apologized for pointing fingers, we all sat in silence and looked at the kitten. Well, *almost* silence. The kitten sat on my father's lap, getting his ears scratched, and purred so loudly we could all hear him.

Finally, my father asked, "What's his name?"

"I don't know," I said. "So far I haven't come up with anything that fits."

"That's okay, let's wait and see what kind of name grows on him," suggested my mother.

Finally, Lin asked what we were all wondering. "Do you think he got into the dollhouse by himself?"

We all laughed at the thought, but it was uneasy laughter. None of us were really convinced of a good answer.

"Time to clean up," called my mother, and the moment was broken. We had to get up and go about our tasks for the evening.

Little did we know, but the kitten was just getting started.

CHAPTER FOUR

Will got the job at National Cash Register—NCR. He worked three days a week and came home pretty full of himself. He loved telling us stories about life at "The Register." He got to know many of the workers and overseers by running messages and parts across the grounds. NCR was a huge complex, with more than ten large buildings. Rail tracks ran alongside several of the buildings for unloading materials and loading up cash registers that shipped out across the country. The grounds and buildings were kept spotless by an army of gardeners and janitors. Will began offering up bits of housekeeping advice to my mother, which quickly stopped when she asked him to demonstrate.

Often, in the evenings around the supper table, Will interjected into the conversation words of wisdom that he'd gleaned from his day at NCR. The first time this happened my father was in the middle of talking about a particularly tough stump removal.

"The world loves the man who works and keeps on working, and still keeps on working, and still keeps on working, but it has no use for the quitter," Will said.

We all sat there in stunned silence, staring at the person who used to be my brother. Jasper alone seemed uninterested. He just sat and swiped at his nose.

The silence was broken by my mother. "My, oh my. Such a brilliant boy," she teased. "You must take after me."

Will just grinned.

My dad chuckled. "Looks like I'm in the right profession," he said. "As a farmer, the work is never done." Then he threw back his head and belly-laughed.

After a while we came to expect Will's wisdom. Someone would mention a challenge of the day and the conversation stopped and everyone looked at Will.

"Wait to do a thing one hundred percent right and you'll accomplish nothing," he would say.

Every once in a while, Will got himself in trouble. One time he quoted, "Do what you are asked to do. Then make suggestions." That phrase would come back to haunt him again and again and again.

Besides Will's newfound wisdom, little else was entertaining in my life. Summer in Ohio was usually very hot and humid, but bearable. This summer it rained. It rained, and rained, and then it rained.

25

On yet another Saturday filled with rain, my parents went out to visit friends. The five of us kids were left at home to tend to the livestock and chores. Our work didn't keep us busy for long enough. Lin, Will, and I ended up looking out the front window—watching the rain. There would be no exploring, no experiments today.

I let out a sigh and went to my father's big chair, flopped down, and began studying the ceiling. Will and Lin continued to look out at the rain. Then Will straightened up a bit. He asked Lin, "Do you see Daisy?"

"Yep."

Our parents had taken the team with the buggy, leaving Daisy, our horse, alone. Daisy was a Morgan horse, small but sturdy and even-tempered. Although she was a pretty reddish-brown color, today she looked almost black, soaked by the rain. She stood in the middle of the horse field with her head down and water dripping off her nose. She looked miserable, especially since she was standing in and surrounded by mud.

"I gotta idea," breathed Will.

Will and Lin put their heads together and started to whisper. As Will explained, Lin grew excited. As they continued to scheme, Lin's arms started flapping up and down. Annie and Jasper, who'd been playing together in the living room, recognized the signs, exchanged panicked glances, and scurried upstairs. They did not want to be anywhere near Lin and Will when they finally figured out their plan.

Me? I couldn't wait to see what was going to happen. I sat up in my father's chair and waited. I could tell this was going to be good. Finally, Lin turned and looked at me, "If you want to come with us, better get some pants on. Meet us outside by the horse field."

I ran up to my room, pulled a pair of Will's old pants out from where I kept them under my bed. My mother tried to keep me in dresses, but I just didn't see the point. Pants let me run with the boys. I put them on, along with a pair of Will's old shoes. I added my oldest shirt, then clomped downstairs and out into the rain.

By the time I got to the field, Lin and Will were already there. Will said, "We figured you could go first since you're the lightest." Although that was what Will said, I knew that what he meant was, "If someone is going to die from this idea, it may as well be you." That was fine with me. I was used to being the one they tried out their ideas on.

Then Lin explained, "We're going to do some mud-sledding." He took a breath and added, "On this." He held out a big, metal bowl.

My heart stopped. They had gone too far this time. *This* wasn't just any bowl. "This" was our mother's new biscuit bowl. She loved her bowl and had used it almost daily since she got it. Nobody, but nobody touched it but her. And now Lin was trying to hand it to me—to ride in.

"No way!"

"Nothing else is big enough; it's perfect. It's okay, nothing will happen to it," Will said. I almost laughed at Will because something always happened when Will was involved.

Then Lin started to explain what they had in mind, and it sounded so good it was almost worth the risk of being skinned alive.

"Just hold on tight when we slap Daisy on the rear, and it'll be the greatest ride you've ever had." I looked at the horse. She seemed willing, and her tail was nice and long. The field was perfect: slick wet mud from fence to fence, with just a few tufts of grass here and there. It really sounded like fun, and our parents weren't due back for hours. Lin and Will were counting on me, and besides, I could blame *them* if anything happened.

"Okay, I'll do it," I said, and before I had a chance to catch my words, they had me in the field. We walked over to Daisy, who, with our approach, looked both less willing and more nervous. But she stood still. After I said "Hi" and petted her, I sat down in the bowl behind her and grabbed on tight to her tail. When I nodded, Will smacked her butt. She took off with a start, and I pitched forward.

I was so surprised that I forgot to let go of her tail for about ten feet. That whole time, Daisy dragged me—face first—through the mud. At least I kept my mouth shut. My eyes, too. Finally I let go and slid to a stop.

Lin and Will ran over to me, and I looked up smiling. "This could work. Maybe next time I should kneel so that I can lean back a bit."

It wasn't long before the three of us had the whole process down to a fine art. Kneel in the bowl—hook your feet over the back rim—grab onto Daisy's tail—and lean back. Daisy even got into the act and started to run once she felt the pressure on her tail. She raced around the field at a pretty good clip, kicking up mud as she went.

We held on till we lost our balance or fell off from laughing too hard. We would have kept on mud-sledding all afternoon, but after about an hour there was an accident. Will was going along pretty good when suddenly there was a muffled clunk. The bowl struck a rock and pitched Will off to the side. Although he got banged up a bit, he was still in one piece. By the time we got there, he had already scrambled over to the bowl.

The bowl. The *dented* bowl. We were all going to die.

"What are we going to do?" I squeaked.

Lin took the bowl from Will's hand and looked it over. Not only was it dented, but we'd scratched it up pretty badly as well.

"Okay," he finally said, "I'll go pound out the

dent. Lee, you polish it up the best you can." He stopped and looked at me kinda funny. He turned and looked at Will. "Well, I'll be!"

"What?" I asked.

"You're full of mud."

I almost made a smart remark, but then I took a good look at him and Will, and I saw what he meant. *They* were full of mud—covered head to toe. The gooey mud had caked on to where we didn't even look like people. It had been raining the whole time we'd been playing. You'd think the rain would have washed off the mud, but all it did was make us a nice, shiny, lumpy brown. There was just too much mud for the rain to deal with. We'd have to take care of the mud before the bowl, but there was no place on the farm we could get it all off.

"We could go to the pond," I offered. Our grandparents lived close by, and they had a pond.

"No way," Will countered. "Grandma and Granddad would know we were there before we ever reached the pond, then we'd have to explain what we were up to."

"We're going to have to go to the river," Lin concluded with a sigh. The Mad River was about a mile or so north of us.

"How long do we have until Mom and Dad get home?" Will asked.

"They won't be home till just before nightfall, so that's not a problem, but we'd still better get going.

Lee, you check on Annie and Jasper, then we'll go."

I slogged up toward the front of the house. Our dog Beans, who had been sleeping along the side of the house, let out a startled yip and ran under the porch. I hollered for Annie and Jasper. There was no way I was going to get close to the house. They peeked out the front door with wide eyes. The two were fine, although they seemed a bit unsettled as they stood at the front door looking out at me, the mud girl. I didn't even bother to tell them that they couldn't say anything to our parents. They knew.

"We'll be back in an hour or so, once we clean up," I said.

The two nodded up and down, then shut the door. I could see their noses pressed to the front window as we walked down the lane.

Once we got to the road we headed towards the river. Then Lin got to thinking it wouldn't do for the neighbors to see us like this, so we moved off to the side and started tramping through the woods the best we could. Sometimes we ventured across the road to try the other side. Ohio was full of swamps where the farmers hadn't gotten in and taken over, so the going was slow. After about fifteen minutes a buggy went by. We hadn't heard them until they were close, so we just stopped in our tracks.

They hurried along at quite a pace, so we didn't think they saw us. Another buggy happened along a while later. Again we froze. As we got closer to the river, the buggies appeared more often, and we opted to hunch down and move ahead rather than hide. We didn't have the time to waste; the day was moving on.

Once we got to the river, it was a delight to jump in and wash off all the mud. It had been raining all day, but summer in Dayton was still really hot. The mud was starting to itch like crazy.

We headed home at a quick trot, and then Lin set to work in the barn fixing the bowl. Will did the evening chores, and I attempted to fix dinner with Annie's help. When Lin came in with the bowl, he took over making dinner and then set the table. I worked at polishing the bowl. When I finished it looked a lot better, but definitely not as good as new.

What to do? What could we do? We put the bowl away in the cabinet and determined to pretend we never touched it.

When we prayed with Jasper and Annie before they went to bed that evening, the three of us were at the top of their list. They seemed convinced that our lives were in need of fervent prayer. Strangely, that wasn't comforting. Just before dark our parents walked in the door. Their day had been great, and they told us all about it. When they asked us what we had done all day, Lin said, "We did all our chores."

"Is that all?" asked my father.

"Well, we went swimming at the river," Will offered.

"Swimming in the rain. That sounds . . . different," said my father as he eyed us. I could feel the pressure building. I couldn't take it. Our parents had always told us, "Fess up when you mess up. Honesty was always better than running."

I looked at Will. He did a quick headshake, No. I looked at Lin. I could tell he was starting to crack, too.

I opened my mouth, just as Lin blurted out, "We dented Mom's bowl."

"What?" she asked.

"Your bowl, we used it to ride in the mud . . ." and with that, the three of us proceeded to spill everything.

Both parents were quiet for a long minute after we finished our story.

"Well," my father finally began, "I'm glad you said something and didn't try to hide it. That's good. But you all know how special that bowl was to your mother."

"I know, we know, Dad. And Mom, we're really sorry. We fixed it the best we could."

At Lin's apology, Will got up and retrieved the bowl. He held it out for our mother to inspect.

She took it from him and looked at it, turned it over in her hands and ran her hand along the bottom. The three of us watched in silence.

"It's not as bad as you made it sound," she said. "But you three still get to weed the garden Monday morning."

The garden was huge, giving us enough vegetables for the entire year. Monday would not be boring.

Then she sighed, set the bowl aside and smiled, "So, was it fun?"

With that, we settled down beside them and told them all about our adventure.

When our father heard about our trip to the river he laughed and said, "I wonder how many people you scared to death."

The boys and I just looked at each other and shrugged. No one in the buggies seemed to pay us any mind.

CHAPTER FIVE

A person can do a whole lot of thinking while weeding. Since the garden was massive, I had a bunch of time to think. I remembered something that had come up a few weeks before—the remark Mr. Stanley had made about the "flying boys." I had heard talk about two brothers who were working on flying, but it was mostly jokes. I hadn't thought much of it; nobody did. Every once in a while, Dad read us a snippet from the paper about the two Dayton brothers and their experiments. All the paper said was that there was nothing to it.

I asked Lin what he thought. Turns out Mr. Stanley's remark had stuck with him as well. He had done some asking around. Someone showed him a newsletter written by a local beekeeper, from a year back. The newsletter talked about the brothers and said they had really flown—the beekeeper had seen them.

"The paper says they are out at Huffman Prairie,

just off the interurban line at Simms Station," Lin concluded.

Lin, Will, and I decided that after we conquered the garden, we would see if we could find out more. With a goal in mind the weeds didn't stand a chance—we finished up in a flash. After a quick check-in with our mother, we headed out.

The hike to the closest interurban station wasn't too far. Will, the breadwinner of the bunch, sprang for our fare. I'd only ridden on the interurban twice, so that alone made the day pretty exciting. Its two cars sat on a track like a train, but instead of an engine, long poles connected it to electric wires that ran above, like a trolly. The trains connected Dayton to all the towns around us, making Cincinnati, Columbus, Xenia, and even Toledo and Lake Erie, accessible.

The first train, heading into Dayton, came by almost as soon as we arrived. Before we got on, Lin thought to ask which direction Simms Station was. The Station was the other direction, away from Dayton. We waited about twenty more minutes until the right train came along. Once on board, our ride was quick. Less than five minutes later, we reached our destination.

We got off the interurban and it rumbled away. The station wasn't much more than a little wood platform with a small sign that said, "Simms Station." The road stretched out in either direction, empty.

Now that we were there we weren't sure where to go.

Across the road, which we later found out was named Dayton-Springfield Pike, stood a barbed-wire fence in front of a row of trees. Past the trees was a large field filled with cows and horses. On the far side of the field was a small barn. The field was pretty big, about a hundred acres, filled with tiny islands of grass in an ocean of mud. Almost in the middle was a single, large tree—a thorn tree. It did not look like a place that people would try to fly, not that I had any idea about what a flying place should look like.

We were just about to start down the road to investigate further when Will noticed that there were people in the barn. We couldn't see much because of the trees, so after checking up and down the road to make sure no one was looking, we went through the fence and crept to the edge of the field.

From our new vantage point, we could see into the barn. Sure enough, three men were working inside. Two were dressed like they were going to church, which was odd because it was hot outside. The other man was in shirtsleeves. What they were working on looked big and flat and white.

"Strange," said Will.

I was about to suggest that we should go when Lin said, "It's so strange, I bet these are the right guys."

Oh great, we were going to spy on a couple of odd

eggs. It wasn't like we could walk over and ask what they were doing, and we couldn't very well sneak across the field. This was as good as it gets, and it wasn't much. Besides, there were three men, not two. We'd been told about two brothers. I was ready to look elsewhere, but I knew that if I said we should leave, the boys would just dig in their heels to stay. Instead, I decided to show how stupid staying around was by suggesting the impossible, "Well, let's just go take a closer look."

Lin and Will looked at me, and then each other. I couldn't believe it. They were considering my idea. I thought, *Why do I hang out with these two?* They thought I was serious. Lin looked up and down the tree line, thinking. Then he turned around and whispered, "If we follow the trees down past where the cattle are grazing, we can sneak across the field and the cows will hide us. The men will never see us. Besides, they seem pretty busy inside."

When Lin set his mind to something, not much would change it. And just because I thought he was nuts didn't mean I shouldn't follow him. So we set out down the tree line. The cows paid us no mind as we crawled behind them on all fours. When we were about two-thirds of the way across the field, one of the men stepped outside and walked to an odd, tripod structure made up of tall poles standing beside the barn. He began to fiddle with something at its base. We all flattened out as best we could on the ground.

I say best we could because the ground was full of big tufts of grass, mud, and cow pies. The grass stood up above the mud like little islands, and the cow pies were scattered throughout. Trying not to twist an ankle or slip on a fresh pie, our trip across the field was tricky. The flopping down part was downright complicated. I did the best, ending up with each hand and both knees firmly planted on a little grassy island, straddling the mud. Lin managed to get down with just a minor slip. Will's encounter with a cow pie ensured that we would be walking home instead of riding on the interurban.

The man finally went back inside, and the three of us continued across the field. Once on the other side, we were able to sneak alongside the barn. If one of the men had ventured outside we would have been caught, but no one did.

Once next to the barn, we could get a better look at the tall structure that the man had been poking around. *Very* strange. It was made up of four long poles, standing twenty feet high and connected at the top. On the ground was the biggest weight I'd ever seen, with a rope attached to it. The rope ran up to a pulley that was suspended just below where the four poles came together. Then, the rope ran down to a pulley on the ground and along the side of a really long metal rail.

We crept alongside the rail and Lin said, "Sakes alive, that's got to be at least fifty feet long." He looked up at the poles and then at the weight. Then he scratched his head, "Wonder what this is for?"

Will and I could only shrug, because we had no idea.

When we reached the far end of the rail we discovered yet another pulley. *What was it with pulleys this summer?* I wondered. With all the pulleys Lin should have been in heaven, but instead he was stumped. We all were.

Inside the barn the men were talking. We moved closer to the barn so that we could hear them better. We sat down at the back end of the structure, where we could hear and still not be seen.

They seemed to be friendly with each other and working hard on what they were doing. They kept talking about struts and elevators, rudders and ribs. After a while Will asked, "Do you think this is the right place? It doesn't seem like what they're talking about has a thing to do with flying."

"You're right," I agreed quickly. Then I voiced my concerns, "and there's three of them, not two like what we've heard. We've always heard about *two* flying brothers."

Lin was silent for a few minutes, and I could tell he was disappointed. Finally he let out a sigh and said, "Well, we might as well go. Maybe the brothers are down the road a ways."

Then, just as we were getting up to leave, one of the men inside the barn said, "Well, Charlie, looks like we'll be ready to fly this Friday, sound good to you?"

We all grinned. We not only had the right folks, we knew when they'd be trying to fly.

About that time the wind shifted, and Lin and I got a good whiff of Will. We looked at him and he said, "What?" He smelled nasty. It was time to go home. We sneaked back across the field and then headed west down the road. Funny thing, it was almost faster to walk than it had been taking the interurban.

The whole way home we talked about what we had seen and heard. None of us understood the things the men were talking about. The tall thing was a mystery as well. What pestered us the most was wondering where they would be flying.

"It couldn't be that field," Will reasoned. "With the cows and the lumps, not to mention the thorn tree in the middle, it'd be impossible."

Lin and I agreed. We just started up the lane to our farm when Annie came running up, stopping us short. The poor thing looked fit to be tied. "Lee, your kitten is stuck up a tree and I can't get him to come down!"

CHAPTER SIX

Annie seemed pretty shook up, but then again she was nine. At nine, everything's a big deal. Since I was twelve, I didn't get shook. I figured cats climb trees because they're cats. Of course, my kitten wasn't quite normal, so I said, "Show me where he is, Annie, and we'll get him down."

The three of us followed her to the big oak tree by the house. There, twenty feet up in the air, the grey kitty peered down.

Okay, *now* I was a bit nervous. He was a long way up, and he wasn't all that smart. That whole thing with the dollhouse—the more I watched him, the more convinced I became that he mashed his own self into it. He also mashed himself into a tin of soda crackers. Then there was the time I found him wedged between our sofa and the wall...upside down.

The kitty also chased our dog, Beans. Anytime Beans came within sight of the kitty, the kitty would hiss and charge him. The first time this happened,

Beans good-naturedly held his ground—let's say "Hi" to the new guy and all. The kitten ran at him, jumped and landed on his back, yowling like a crazy thing. Beans panicked. He let out a yelp and ran around the yard twice before he shook the beast loose.

Since then, when he sees the kitten, he runs for cover with his tail between his legs. Stranger still, the kitten is scared to death of mice; any time he sees a mouse he hides. That's how he ended up wedged behind the couch. Now here he was up a tree.

I started toward the tree, but Lin stopped me, "You're in a dress; I'll go." With that he began to climb. As he moved up the tree he spoke softly to the kitty. (He was still "kitty" since we hadn't found a name that suited him.) As Lin climbed, the kitten looked on with great interest, not looking a bit flustered. But as Lin got closer, the kitten backed out onto the branch. Lin climbed up eye-to-eye with the kitten, stopped, and smiled. Slowly he reached out his hand.

The kitten, as if it was all a game, ran up to Lin, turned just before he could be reached, then ran off the end of the branch at top speed. We all watched in stunned silence as the kitten leapt off the branch, his legs outstretched as if he was trying to fly. It didn't work. It seemed like a long time passed before he landed.

He didn't land well. The kitten landed on his back, and it was horrifying. The poor thing writhed in pain and let out a hair-raising scream. I scooped him up and held him close, but he just kept on yowling. Will and Annie looked on in shock. I was shaking and fighting back the tears.

As soon as Lin came down the tree, he came up to me and said, "We'd best pray for him." I relaxed a bit and thought, *I should have thought about that.* We prayed for the kitten, thanking God that he would be all better. Then I just held him and rocked him. Within a few minutes the kitten quieted down.

We took him into the kitchen and told my mother what had happened, but by this time the kitten was calm and beginning to purr. We told her about the tree and Lin, then the mad dash off the branch, and the ultimate fall. We finished by recounting our prayer. At first she thought we were pulling her leg, but after we dragged her outside and told her the whole thing yet again, she shook her head and said, "Better keep a close watch on him tonight. Cats don't do well falling from high places; their bones are too delicate."

She took him from me and examined him closely. "On his back, are you sure he landed on his back? I've never heard of such a thing."

The kitten slept in my room that night. Every once in a while I would wake up and check on him. He was sleeping so soundly that I poked him a few times just to make sure he was still alive. Once I poked him he'd start to purr and I'd go back to sleep. The next day the kitten was as good as new, bouncing around and getting stuck in odd places. This had us all puzzled. The Gypsies said he was special, but this was just plain odd.

But there was too much to do to worry. June was slipping by at lightning speed. Friday the 23rd, the day that held the promise of flying brothers, would be coming soon.

CHAPTER SEVEN

Friday morning I woke up early. Lin and I planned on getting our chores done as soon as possible so we could go out to the field where the men would be trying to fly. Will had to work at NCR. He had already left, slogging off to work, looking dismayed that he was gainfully employed. I did my daily cleaning chores around the house and then headed outside to feed Pork our table scraps.

I walked around the corner of the house, and there, much to my surprise, was my sister Annie, lurking in the bushes. This was not an everyday occurrence. Annie doesn't lurk. She moves about in a graceful manner, with an ease of motion and posture befitting a lady. This morning she was on her knees hiding behind a bush. Needless to say, she had my attention. Because she was so engrossed in what she was doing, she didn't see me at first. When she did, she quickly put her finger to her mouth, "Shhhh."

I dropped down on my knees and scooted in beside her. "What are you doing?" I whispered.

"Beans has my sweater," she whispered back. Although Beans is technically the family dog, he just barely puts up with us kids. Most days he accompanies my father while he goes about his work on the farm, lending a helping paw when he can. The dog got the name Beans because that is about the strongest swear word my father uses. Apparently he uses it a whole lot in the field. After a while the dog started answering to it, thus his name—Beans.

Beans had his reasons for being wary of us kids. Can't say I blame him. Lin and Will and I, would sometimes utilize Beans's services in our quest for scientific enlightenment. Unfortunately once or twice Beans's hair got a bit singed—but only here and there. A few other times speed and sudden stops were involved—but nothing life-threatening.

There *was* an unfortunate incident with his tail as well. Beans failed to see the greatness of our experiments and, sadly, lacked a sense of humor. Consequently, we seldom enjoyed his company. He does like Jasper, however. That's because Beans eats anything Jasper has. And I do mean *anything*. Beans has the eating habits of a goat, stopping just short of tin cans.

And now, judging from her state of panic, Beans was eating Annie's sweater. Because of her alarm, I assumed it was her new sweater from our grandma.

It was a beautiful white-with-lace-and-pretty-pearl-buttons sweater, and grandma had made it just for Annie. I couldn't imagine how Beans got a hold of it, but I could clearly imagine him chewing it up and making a mess. She needed help—big sister to the rescue! This felt good; I was good. "Where is he?" I asked.

"Under the porch, see?"

I looked real close and there was Beans' nose sticking out from under the porch. No sweater hung out from his mouth, which was a good sign. I crept a bit closer and noticed a paw sticking out, but what caught my eye was just above Beans's paw, on his leg. I looked back at Annie and whispered, "He's *wearing* your sweater?"

"Yes," she said, like I should have known or in some way expected this. "I put it on him."

I looked at her for a moment. In some odd way, it made sense. Annie was always trying to dress up the barn cats. She'd sneak up on them while they were sleeping, bundle them in a blanket, and then haul them to her room. Once locked in her lair, they were dressed up in baby clothes and stuffed into her baby carriage, pinned in place by baby blankets.

"How did you get a hold of him?"

"He was asleep and I sat on him. I thought he'd look nice in the sweater, but then he ran off before I could get him up to my room."

I thought, *Dumb move. Smart dog.*

Okay, I understood. The cats were Annie-smart. Not only could they manage to get away from her, but as they dashed to freedom the offending clothes usually flew in all directions, leaving a trail of bonnets and bunting down the hallway. With Beans, the sweater fit too snugly and he couldn't shake it off.

We sneaked a few feet closer. Now that I had a better look at him, I could tell he wasn't really pleased with the predicament he was in. Both of them needed help. I whispered, "Come with me," and backed away from the porch.

I snitched a bit of crust from a cooling pie in the summer kitchen, and then we went back outside. I made sure the door banged behind me and called out, "Beans, scraps!" There was a bit of noise and Beans bolted around the corner, eager for a handout. When he saw Annie, his tail drooped and he screeched to a halt. Before he finished his turn to make a getaway, I tackled him.

He looked at me like, "Do you see what she did to me?" He was a big dog, red and shaggy with big brown eyes—a rough and tough kind of dog. And now Beans was wearing a little white lacy sweater that stretched across his back and rode up his front legs. His long fur stuck out at odd angles around the neck and through the lace. Beans was not a happy dog.

Quickly, I gave him the piece of crust I had in my hand. As he chewed I adjusted my grip so that I could sit on him. I reckoned if it worked for Annie, it'd work for me. She and I began to wrestle the sweater off him. You would think he would be glad we were helping him and offer assistance. Instead, he wiggled and fought. I have no idea how Annie ever managed to get her sweater on the animal. She must have bent his legs in ways they'd never gone before. That she did it alone gave me a new respect for her abilities. To get it off took both of us. She worked the sweater and I tried to get the dog's parts pointing in the right direction. We finally disconnected the dog from the sweater, and he jumped to his feet and shook himself. He made a noise that sounded like, "Humpf," and then walked away—not bothering to look back. *Honor restored,* I thought.

I looked at the sweater in Annie's hand. Not quite white anymore and a bit stretched out. "Wow," I said. "Would you like me to help you clean that up?" As the words escaped my lips, I realized how foolish they sounded. "Sister to the rescue" had just jumped in way over her head. I was not particularly gifted in the laundry area. In fact, if you wanted new stains, holes, lost buttons, or snags, let me do the washing.

Annie looked at me, managed a smile, and said, "Gee, thanks, Lee, but I think I can take care of this." With a quick hug she was on her way.

Back to the business at hand, I was now officially behind with my chores. Dang! Just as I tackled the breakfast dishes, Lin stuck his head in the kitchen.

"Take your time, Lee," he said. "Dad needs some help this morning. One of the calves is sick." My heart sank, and Lin didn't look too pleased either. "Don't worry," he said, "Dad will let me go just as soon as he can."

"Let me know if I can help out."

"Great," he smiled. "Can you bring a bucket of fresh water out to the barn?" He started to leave, and then stopped and said, "You know, you're okay, even if you *are* a girl."

I looked at him as he walked away. A girl— pshaw! He knew I could keep up with him any day.

Before too long I was running to keep up with him. It was early afternoon, and the calf was doing better. My father had given Lin his leave. After Lin came and found me, we set out at a trot towards the field.

"Hurry up," he yelled over his shoulder. "I don't want to miss anything." But by the time we made it through the fence and crept through the trees to the edge of the field, it was clear we were too late to see anything.

The three men were there and had a big machine outside of the barn, but they were putting it away. As we watched from the cover of the trees, they disconnected a piece from the front of the machine and another from the back. Then they took the middle part, the biggest piece—which was two long, horizontal wings covered with cream-colored cloth—and put it in the barn. The other two pieces followed.

We watched in fascination. "I had no idea that thing was so big," Lin whispered.

"I had no idea they were this serious. That's a lot of work." As we watched, the men let the cows and horses back into the field and then went back into the barn.

"Well, that's it," Lin said. "We need to come back again—soon. I gotta see this."

As we headed home both of us were silent for a while. Then I said, "You know, that's no air balloon. These men are really trying to fly."

Up until now the only "flying" that had been done was with huge balloons. Anything outside of balloons was considered impossible. Sure, there had been men who had tried to make a flying machine—scientists and big institutions—but no one was successful. We couldn't imagine that these men, bicycle mechanics, had a chance. But we couldn't stay away until we knew for sure.

We made our plans to go back.

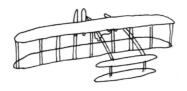

CHAPTER EIGHT

We journeyed out to the field two more times with no reward. By this time June had slipped into July. As we headed down the now familiar road, I began to grump. "It's hot . . . this is stupid . . . and why are we doing this?" Both the boys were quiet as I continued my irritating solo.

Finally Will turned to me and said, "Look, little sister, you don't have to tag along if you don't want to. No one's forcing you."

That stopped me. After all, I was the little sister. I knew I'd better pipe down. They didn't bring up the little sister factor unless I was being especially annoying. I shut my mouth and stretched out my legs to keep pace. We planned on climbing a tree for a better look once we got there, and Lin didn't want to have to rescue me, so I was wearing Will's old pants and shoes. The shoes were way too big, so keeping pace was a bit difficult for me. No more complaining, though. I might be the little sister, but today I was one of the guys.

We never got the chance to climb a tree. Just after we negotiated the fence and made our way through the trees to the edge of the field, a sound caught our attention. There was a sputtering and then steady racket as an engine caught. We looked across the field. There, sitting just below the tall poles, sat the flying machine. They had put it back together. A motor that sat on the bottom wing just off center looked to be connected to two long, thin, gigantic wooden pinwheels. Located behind either side of the big parallel wings, the pinwheels slowly started to spin. While we watched, they spun faster until they were just a blur. Lying next to the motor, right in the middle of the wing, was one of the men dressed in a suit.

Lin and I looked at each other. "They're going to give it a try," Lin exclaimed. With that we all leaned forward in anticipation.

As we watched, the other two men stepped back, each holding the machine by a wingtip to steady it. Will started to make a crack about the thing being unsteady and whispered, "If that thing can't stay upright on the ground, how can they expect it to fl . . . . "

He was cut short when the big weight, which had been at the top of the poles, came crashing down. As it did, the machine shot forward. Then the impossible happened. It left the ground. As we watched, the machine went from seeming awkward and strange, to looking like a beautiful, graceful bird.

I don't think any of us breathed as we watched it rise in the air and come straight towards us. The three of us stood up and watched it for what seemed like forever, but it was probably only about twenty seconds. Suddenly Lin realized we were out in the open. "Duck!" he yelled. As we scrambled for cover, the plane turned. Just past us, it landed. The whole thing didn't last long, less than a minute, but it was remarkable.

As we watched, the other two men headed out to the field while the man who flew—yes, he did fly the machine—shut off the engine and got up. The three men began talking excitedly, walking around the machine, shaking one part and poking at another. Then they began to move the big contraption back towards the barn. It must have weighed a lot. It took all three of them working together to move the machine across the lumpy ground. Making it even more difficult, the machine wasn't on wheels, but skids like a sled.

The sat still as stones, not wanting to miss a moment. I think all our minds were on overload; none of us had yet said a word, well, besides "duck." The men got the thing back to the barn and started taking it apart. Finally, Lin began inching his way back into the woods. We sat there with our backs to trees, just looking at each other and grinning.

Will finally said what we all were thinking: "They can fly!" With that, we started jumping around, too excited to sit still.

As we headed home to tell our family all about the day, our words tumbled over one another. We talked over everything we saw. Something that had us puzzled were the skids that the airplane sat on. I guessed they used the skids because of the lumpy ground. Or maybe they had enough to deal with just figuring out flying, without having to worry about their machine rolling away.

"Maybe they want to stop fast since they're surrounded by barbed wire and there's a thorn tree in the middle of the field," Will offered. Thinking back to our first impression of the field, he probably had the right idea.

With that mystery solved to our satisfaction, we went back to the big picture. The airplane really worked. It was in the air, and not just because it was catapulted off. It flew under its own power. We had seen what few even considered possible; we had seen our first airplane.

CHAPTER NINE

The days that followed were almost full enough to crowd the flying brothers from our minds—almost. Mr. Patterson, the president of NCR, arrived back in Dayton on July 3, after a yearlong, around-the-world tour. The entire city of Dayton came out to see him. Since we'd been bugging her for days, my mother brought us downtown to see all the hoopla.

Downtown streets were decorated with NCR's colors—gold and burgundy. Mr. Patterson and his wife rode in the back of an open carriage, smiling and waving like they were royalty. Flanking the Pattersons were the mayor and several of the town council. After the carriage passed by, my mother shook her head and said, "That man is certainly the biggest toad in this puddle."

Will dug in his heels at the comment. "But Mom," he said, "Mr. Patterson's not full of himself. He made the factory a nice place to work and he gives us malted milk."

She looked at him. "I can see he made a friend for life with the malted milk," she said. "He *did* teach you, 'Do what you're asked to do. Then make suggestions.' Guess I owe him for that."

Will smiled but in a pained sort of way. That had become our mother's answer to Will's many, "But, Mom, why can't we . . . ?"

The next morning, I brought the grey kitten into the kitchen from outside. It was time for his morning milk. He came running in with his tail up in the air and frisked about impatiently while I poured milk in a bowl. He lapped it up eagerly, and after he finished I scooped him up to put him back out. He mewed in pain. I looked at him closer. When I saw what was bothering him, I yelled, "Mom!"

Since she was right behind me, she almost dropped the bowl she was stirring.

"Lordy, Lee, don't be doing that to me. You nearly scared me to death. What's wrong with you?"

"It's not me, it's the kitten." I showed her his side.

"Oh, honey," she said. "It looks like an owl tried to get him."

Along the kitten's side, a big hole was ripped in his skin, exposing the muscles underneath. I could see his belly and his leg all the way down past where it bent from the inside. She looked him over carefully, which he didn't seem to mind at all. In fact, by this time the silly thing was purring, enjoying the extra attention.

"Nothing's damaged on the inside," she said, "it's just the big hole. Looks like the owl got him and then he wriggled free. His loose skin saved him." She set him down and watched him walk around. "Let's just keep him in the house while he heals up so he doesn't get all dirty inside."

She went into the spring room and got a basket. I lined it with an old towel, and we gently set the kitten inside.

At breakfast, we told my father all about what had happened. He asked to see the kitten and closely examined him. My father began to laugh.

"I've never seen anything like this," he said. "First the tree and then an owl . . . ."

I stared at him, wondering why he would find my kitten's abundant misfortunes so funny.

He looked at me and said, "I know your cat's name."

"You do?"

"Oh, yeah. His name is Eutychus."

I couldn't help frowning. *Yoo-ti-kus,* I thought. *That's an odd name.*

The silence from his announcement was broken when my mother started laughing. "Sakes alive, Leo, that *is* that kitten's name. It's perfect."

The rest of us were not getting the humor. My father smiled at her. "Rosie, can you go get my Bible so I can show these kids what I'm talking about?"

She was back in the room with the book in her hand almost before he'd finished asking. We waited while he turned the pages in the big book. My mother was leaning over his shoulder saying, "It's before Paul was arrested, but after Athens."

Then my father said, "Here it is. In the book of Acts, chapter 20, verse 9, 'And there sat in a window a certain young man named Eutychus, being fallen into a deep sleep: and as Paul was long preaching, he sunk down with sleep, and fell down from the third loft, and was taken up dead.'

"This guy fell out of a window and died. The next few verses go on to tell about Paul praying for the lad and in verse 12, 'And they brought the young man alive, and were not a little comforted.' Doesn't that sound like our kitten?"

My mother leaned into him and said, "Now tell them what the name means."

My father chuckled. "That's the best part," he said. "God must have a great sense of humor, because Eutychus means 'lucky.'"

We burst into laughter. All the while Eutychus, who had climbed up onto my father's open Bible, looked on with a mild interest.

Then our father looked around and said, "I can't believe this. You all forgot, didn't you?" We looked at him blankly. "What day is it?" There were more blank looks. "I'll give you a hint—trees."

All of the sudden I understood. "We get measured today!"

CHAPTER TEN

In the courtyard of our farm each child in the Twist household had his or her own tree. Every year on the Fourth of July, our father stood each of us up against our personal tree and notched our height into the trunk. Next to the notch we then carved the date. This time I carved out "1905." In one short year, I had grown three inches. Will, for once, grew the most, beating out Lin by shooting up more than six inches.

"We'll have to stop feeding you or you'll outgrow the house," my father teased him. Will strutted around and Lin grumbled. I was a bit distressed. Already taller than I thought right, my three inches were not welcome.

Once we were measured and the date was carved into each tree, we went into the house and got ready for the day. Since it was the Fourth of July, we cleaned up the dishes and packed the abundance of food my mother and Annie had made, and then headed over to our grandparents' house to celebrate the Fourth.

Just to the north of us was the original Twist family homestead. My grandparents and my father's oldest brother, Albert, his wife, and their six children, lived there. Four more sets of aunts and uncles lived within a mile, each with its own crop of offspring. Only one of my uncles lived outside the area, the youngest, David. When Uncle David turned nineteen, he headed west in search of adventure. He was the only uncle on my father's side I didn't know. Every once in a while, grandma and granddad got a letter from him, telling of the latest adventure. He was the only Twist who wouldn't be at the Fourth of July celebration.

All in one place, the Twist family made for quite a time. The women promptly went to the kitchen, catching up, and putting the picnic food together. The men sat on the porch and talked about crops and livestock. The rest of us were left to our own devices.

Not counting babies and toddlers, there were more than twenty cousins. The farm had a big, spring-fed pond. It stayed cool throughout the summer and was a favorite place to play. A big tree with a long rope attached stood beside the pond, so that we could swing into the water. Cannonballs off the rope developed into a contest, and soon the water fights and dunking began.

Ernest, one of my cousins, found a snake and

started chasing whoever would run. First on his list of targets was Annie. *Bad idea,* I thought. I talked Lin and Will into tying him to a tree. After they'd accomplished their mission, I stuck a frog down Ernest's shirt. Turns out he was not fond of frogs. Ernest begged and pleaded for an hour before someone had mercy on him and untied him.

In the yard in front of the farmhouse, the younger cousins contented themselves with my grand-parents' ancient dog, Molly. She was Beans' mother and as patient a dog as ever was. She spent the entire afternoon being patted, sat on, and having her ears and tail pulled. Strangely enough, she seemed to enjoy the attention. I asked my grandma about it and she smiled and said, "Oh, she loves kids. But after you all leave, she'll sleep for a couple of days."

I spent most of the afternoon with my favorite cousin, Louise. She and I are only two months apart—I'm older. Just like me, Louise would rather spend her days climbing trees and playing with the boys. The only difference is that she can do anything. Louise can cook and sew in a fashion that would make any mother proud. I don't hold that against her.

We climbed up a tree, far from the reaches of Ernest and his reptilian friend, and swapped stories about the summer. Occasionally we'd get down for a dip and then find our way back up the tree.

I'd pretty well forgotten about Ernest. Seems he

hadn't forgotten about me, however. Bent on getting even, he'd collected a batch of strawberries from my grandmother's garden, carefully selecting the oldest and squishiest. Louise and I had just settled back into our tree after a swim when, *splat!* I got hit on the side of my head with a strawberry. *Yeech!*

For the next several minutes Ernest masterfully utilized his slingshot to pelt us with strawberries. To his credit, he's a great shot. He kept us treed for a while. Finally, we made a break for it and dashed to the safety of the pond. For the rest of the day I smelled like strawberries, which wasn't so bad. Better than smelling like a frog.

After a while the big dinner triangle rang out—it was time to eat. The picnic was grand. Three tables were set end to end and laid out with food. All the aunts brought their best dishes, so everything tasted great. Blankets were spread under the trees. We all filled our plates and picked a spot for food and fellowship. I sat down beside my mother, and she smiled in my direction. With a start, she jumped and grabbed my head with both hands. After an intense inspection, then a sniff, she sighed and looked at me.

"Strawberries?" she asked.

"Yes, m'am."

"I don't want to know," she said with a shake of her head. And she began gathering the contents of her plate, which had scattered in the excitement. Guess I missed a strawberry.

We ate 'til we could eat no more. Afterwards, the leftovers were put in the kitchen to be picked at for the rest of the day.

That evening my grandfather built a big bonfire. My uncles began trading stories around the fire. My father told everyone about the kitten, Eutychus. Everyone got a kick out of his misadventures. My grandfather said that when he was a boy he had a dog that was bent for trouble.

"Something probably happened to him when he was born because he was dumber than a box of rocks from the start. He just couldn't stay out of trouble for a minute. He'd always come home smelling like a skunk or with a face full of porcupine needles."

The evening ended early. The next day everyone would be back to work. Even Will, I thought with a sigh. I missed having him around, even if he was my brother.

CHAPTER ELEVEN

Since Mr. Patterson was back in Dayton, he had the folks at NCR hopping. When he first arrived at the factory they rang a big bell, and all the workers poured out of the buildings to greet him. He spoke to the crowd for a while, briefly telling them of the success of his tour and the European branches of NCR. Everyone cheered and then they were dismissed to go back to work. Mr. Patterson went to work as well. Seems he wanted to make up for the time he was away, and his changes were really causing a ruckus.

Mr. Patterson had gotten pretty sick while he was in Europe, so he employed a fitness fellow. Not only did he get better; he felt great. Being the man he was, he decided that everyone else needed to feel as good as he did. He'd even brought along a special athletic trainer from Europe. The day after he returned from Europe, he did a big meeting for all the executives. For the crowd, the trainer, Charles Palmer, had Mr. Patterson do a variety of exercises that he'd been taught. Mr. Patterson really moved! Everyone in the factory talked about it for days.

All the changes kept Will busy running from building to building, carrying messages and packages back and forth. He came home dog-tired each afternoon. Trying to figure out a time for the three of us to go spy on the flying brothers was not working, so Lin and I decided to walk out to the field without him. It'd been more than a week, and we couldn't wait to see the brothers fly again.

When Lin and I arrived in the woods, we found the three men just getting started. We watched as they took the three cloth-covered pieces out of the barn and carefully assembled them. Once finished they set the machine on a small, two-wheel carriage that rode on the rail up next to the poles. After that, they caught a couple of plow horses and tied them by the barn. Once they fitted each of the horses with harnesses, they hooked the horses up to a rope attached to the big weight. Very carefully they coaxed the horses forward, pulling the weight into the air. It looked just like something Lin and Will would do.

The three men worked in concert, one working the horses, one on the rope and the other under the machine. When they were finished, the airplane stood ready to go. But their work wasn't finished. They put the harnesses back in the barn, straightened up their tools, then drove the horses and cattle into an adjoining field. This task was made more difficult by several ornery cows that seemed set on making the men's lives more interesting. They'd head towards the gate, and just before going in, they veered right or left. Once the majority of cows were in, the three men ganged up on the wayward few, ultimately winning the battle. After what seemed to me to be a full day's work, they settled into the real task at hand.

They walked around the machine a few times, checking details here and there. Each man double-checked the other. Finally, one of the brothers turned his cap around backwards and climbed onto the airplane.

Lin and I looked at each other and grinned. "Here they go," I breathed.

This time we knew what to expect. We watched as they started the engines and waited while the two men cleared out of the way. Then we held our breath and the weight dropped. The machine shot forward, then suddenly was airborne—beautiful and graceful once again.

Lin and I were spellbound. Like a bird, the machine seemed to belong in the sky. We could see the man lying on the wing, looking intent but happy.

All at once the airplane started jerking around in the air, up and down, like a bucking horse. Something was very wrong. We could see the man's face, grim with intensity, as he desperately tried to steady the machine. Nothing he did worked.

"No, no!" I whispered desperately as I watched. Then the airplane seemed to pause for a moment in the air, gave a shudder, and dove straight down, crashing into the ground. As the airplane shattered into pieces, the man was thrown through the upper wing.

Before I could react, Lin was on his feet, "Come on!" he yelled. He ran to the field as fast as he could; I followed close behind. We reached the wrecked airplane at the same time as the two men from the barn. The man was still lying where he had fallen. One of the men knelt down and softly said, "Orville, are you all right?"

There was a pause, and Orville said in a somewhat surprised voice, "You know what, I think I am."

The two men checked him head to foot to make sure everything was still attached and nothing was leaking. Orville looked fine, so he was helped to his feet. It was the first time I had a good look at him. He had a big mustache and was tall and slender. He was dressed, as usual, in a suit.

I realized that with the heat and his hard work, his suit was soaked. I glanced over at the other man—same thing. Still, they both managed to look neat, although Orville had a rather beat up look to him. I noticed that his cap was missing. Just then, the other man handed it to him.

About that time a woman came running up, armed with liniment.

"Are you boys all right?" she asked. "Is anyone injured?" She spied Orville and began fussing over him.

Where did she come from? I wondered. The men didn't seem surprised to see her. They obviously knew her.

With Orville taken care of, the man turned and looked at Lin and me. Suddenly I realized we were uninvited guests. These people all knew each other, but we were strangers. Just as I started to panic the man smiled and said, "We were wondering when you were going to stop poking around in the woods and come say 'Hi.' Guess it took something exciting. My name's Wilbur."

He stuck out his hand for us to shake. Wilbur was about the same height as his brother, same build, too, and like his brother he had kind eyes. But Wilbur didn't have a mustache and was wearing a bowler hat.

"Now that you're here," he said, "how about you make yourself useful? We need to get all this back to the barn."

Lin helped the men grab the main section. I grabbed a part of the piece that had once been the front of the machine. I caught my breath. *I'm touching part of an airplane*, I thought. As we made our way towards the barn I asked, "What's this thing called?"

The other man, who later introduced himself as

Charlie Taylor, looked over and said, "That, my friend, is called an elevator."

The men talked about what had happened and what they needed to do to fix it. They were so deep into their conversation that they didn't take any notice as to what was going on in my little world. The excitement about touching a plane was wearing off. The elevator seemed to have a life of its own and fought me every step. Adding to the problem, the ground, with all its bumps, made it practically impossible to walk, especially since I couldn't see my feet. Finally I was so frustrated I cut in, "Gee, why don't you just make this thing bigger?"

I couldn't believe the words really came out of my mouth. I thought, *Did I just say that?* These men were letting us be around them, and I was being a grump. I braced myself for their reaction.

The response was not what I expected. Both men stopped and looked at me. Then they looked at each other and started laughing. Wilbur set his side of the wing down right where he was, then headed back to talk to his brother. Charlie, after setting his side down as well, came over to me.

"We might just do that," he said, and punched me in the shoulder. Then he took the elevator from me and walked it up to the barn, all the while chuckling to himself.

Lin, now without a job, looked at me and shook his head, "Dang, Lee, I thought they were going to row you up Salt River for a minute. I couldn't believe you sassed like that. Good thing they don't know you enough to realize how crabby you were being. But whatever you said, they liked. I just wish I knew what it was."

"Yeah, me, too."

We headed back to the crash site, to where the pieces lay and began to gather more of the scattered parts. As we passed Orville and Wilbur, we heard them chattering excitedly. The woman continued to fuss over Orville. She lived in the neighboring farmhouse, it turned out, and made a practice of watching over the brothers. Whenever there was a rough landing she ran liniment over and tended to their bumps and scratches.

Lin and I cleared the field of the remaining pieces and brought them to the barn. Orville looked up and smiled. "Would you boys like to stay for a while?" he asked.

Lin and I quickly said yes. I was excited at the invite, even if they *did* think I was a boy. I couldn't blame them. I was dressed in my familiar summer garb—Will's clothes. And if they thought I was a boy, who was I to correct them?

After all, they could fly.

CHAPTER TWELVE

That evening the dinner table was buzzing. Lin and I told everyone about the day's exploits. "You should have seen it," said Lin. "First, up in the air and then wham!" With the *wham* Lin hit his fist to his hand and my mother jumped, putting her hand over her mouth. He drew out the suspense a bit, gazing around the dinner table, and then he finally added, "But everyone was okay."

He went on to describe how we ran up to help, carried things to the barn, and hung around afterwards. He didn't say that he had asked an abundance of questions, but I think everyone figured that out on their own.

"In the back, there's a rudder which steers the airplane. In the front there's an elevator to control the up and down. The two long, spinning things behind the wings are called propellers, and they move the plane forward. The wings are made with just a wood frame, and then cloth is stretched over it.

They sewed the material themselves. In fact, they made everything themselves!"

My parents listened in stunned silence. Lin, Will, and I had described the flying machine a few weeks before, but I guess they mostly figured we were just being kids, making more of something than it really was. Now, listening to the description of the crash, my parents could tell that a big machine had indeed been traveling through the air at quite a speed. They appreciated the two brothers' dedication, but the seriousness of the accident was alarming.

"It must have been terrible to see," said my mother. And then she added, "Now, don't any of you get it in your head to ride on one of those things." I thought, *No way that's going to happen, especially after what we saw today.*

I thought about what I had seen happen and all of the sudden I gulped and fought back the tears. It was the first time in all of the excitement that I really thought about the actual crash. It had been horrible to see a man flung through the wing like a rag doll. And watching the airplane splinter around him, I could only imagine that the same thing was happening to him. The whole time we were running up to the wreck, I was sure he was dead. I'd never seen anything like it.

"Come here, Lee," my father said, and I went over and crawled up onto his lap. Now I know I'm twelve years old, halfway to thirteen, but I still love to sit in my daddy's lap. It's one of the nicest, safest places on earth. So there I sat, throughout the rest of the meal, letting my heart quiet down.

"Tell us more, Lin," my mother said.

"Well, one of the men is named Charlie Taylor. He's a mechanic and works for the two brothers. Their name is Wright, Wilbur and Orville Wright. When they're not working on their airplane, they make bicycles. They live in Dayton, over on Third Street."

"Why, they're the Bishop's boys," my mother exclaimed. "I've heard about them. Those poor boys have been laughed at for years. Some folks think they're simpleminded—two bachelors running around flying kites. Just goes to show that people shouldn't judge what they don't understand."

Will had been quiet through dinner. He was pretty upset that he had missed all the excitement. But finally he offered, "I get to work at a big party next Friday. It's going to be a homecoming party for Mr. and Mrs. Patterson out in their place at Far Hills. There's supposed to be more than one band and lots of folks. I'm going to help serve food, and I'll get paid for my time."

"That's great, son, you'll have to tell us all about it." Then my father asked, "How're things going 'round NCR? Are things starting to settle down a bit?"

Will paused for a second, then smiled brightly. "Yep," he said, "things are just great."

I stared at Will, thinking, *I'm sure not convinced; we'll be talking soon.*

Just as we were about to clear the table, my mother spoke up. "I almost forgot," she said. "Please remember to keep the front gate closed from now on. Pork's old enough to come out of her pen, and I'm going to let her out tomorrow."

CHAPTER THIRTEEN

Pork was the baby pig that we kept from our sow's litter. I'd been feeding her scraps since she was itty-bitty. Pork was a great pig. After my mother let her out of her pen, she frisked about the yard, happy to be out with the family. From then on, she greeted me each morning, enthusiastically wagging her entire body and turning in circles as I petted her. As I rubbed her ears, she grunted with delight, rolled onto her back so I could scratch her belly, and gave me a big pig smile.

Any time I walked around the farm, Pork followed me like a puppy. She did the same thing with the whole family, and within a week she had us all by the heartstrings. One night, I caught my father sneaking her a bit of his rhubarb pie after supper. When Jasper started playing fetch with her, I realized that basically, Pork—our pig—had become the family dog.

Beans was handling the whole thing relatively

well, partially because he really liked Pork. Every night after everyone went to sleep, Pork curled up with Beans for the night. Pork would even leave Beans select scraps. And, perhaps most important, Pork took the pressure off Beans being a dog.

The lack of attention Beans experienced was what he had always dreamed of. He was now free to lounge around the farm, sleeping wherever he liked. When he wasn't with my father, he'd lie for hours in the shade, sleeping on his back with his feet in the air. The threat of passing children no longer existed—we were all playing with Pork.

The only fly in Beans's ointment was small, grey and furry: Eutychus. The kitten persisted in tormenting the dog. Since Eutychus was healing up nicely, my mother finally let him out of the house. The kitten was determined to make up for lost time.

Early one afternoon, Will and I sat on the steps of the front porch watching the scene unfold. It was a hot and humid day; the air lay heavy like a blanket and the locusts lazily droned. Beans was fast asleep in the shade of our buggy. Eutychus had spotted him and was closing in on his unsuspecting prey. As we watched, he jumped up on the far side of the buggy and made his way to a spot just above his victim.

Will nudged me. "I almost feel sorry for Beans," he said. "Think we should say something?"

"Naw," I said, not taking my eyes off the action, "it's good for Beans, builds character."

As we watched, the kitten gathered himself up and sprang onto the dog, hissing and yowling. Beans scrabbled from his back to his feet and then jumped straight up in the air, knocking Eutychus off to the side. But he didn't seem to realize he was free from his tormenter. He streaked around the yard with his hair on end, yelping and yipping. Finally he retreated underneath the porch. Pork looked up from where she lay beside me, getting her belly scratched, and gave the dog a welcoming grunt. Then she laid her head back down.

The kitten walked away with his tail in the air and a spring in his step, as if to say, "I rule this land." Everything was quiet again. Only the locusts' hum played on in the day's background.

After we'd finished laughing and I caught my breath, I asked Will, "Now, what's going on where you work?"

"What? Nothing. What do you mean?"

"Will, don't even try it. What's up?"

He sat for a minute, kicking at the dirt. Then he said, "I dunno, it's just not the same anymore. I mean, everyone's all nervous now. Don't get me wrong, Mr. Patterson is really nice and he really cares about stuff." Then he laughed, "They say that one time he was teaching the salesmen, and while he was talking he rubbed red chalk all over his face and started jumping up and down shouting 'dramatize your ideas, dramatize!'"

"No way."

"Oh, yeah."

"Okay, so if he's so great, why are people so nervous? What's the problem?" I asked.

"This guy that Mr. Patterson brought back with him, Charles Palmer, he's something else," Will said with a sigh.

"Something else good or something else bad?"

"Not good, that's for sure. He's supposed to help everyone get in shape and get healthy, but he just walks around eyeballing everyone. Rumor has it that he's even gotten a few men fired because he didn't like their faces. Mr. Patterson really respects him and listens to his advice."

"That is bad, but remember what mom said about rumors—don't jump to conclusions. Okay?"

"Yeah, but it's too bad. Around the factory people are smiling more and meaning it less."

"Yeah, well at least you have that party thing tomorrow," I said, elbowing Will gently.

Will perked up. "I have to get all slicked up, wear a white coat and everything."

"Oh, I see. That's really why you've been so sad," I teased him. "You're going to have to clean up. Yuck, water!" And I gave a full body shudder just for good measure.

Will punched me in the arm and laughed, "Yep, they'd never let *you* into a place like that."

I stuck my tongue out and headed into the house.

I walked in through the kitchen—nothing was going on there. My mother and Annie were out in the summer kitchen. It was too hot. I had no desire to go out and cook. Of course, I *never* had a desire to cook, no matter the temperature. I walked into the parlor and flopped down in my father's big chair. What to do? Let's see . . . my chores were done. There was always more I could do, but I wasn't *that* bored. Lin was working in the potato field with my father. I'd talked to Will. Eutychus was probably out looking for some new and inventive way to have a near-death experience. There was nothing to do.

Nothing. I sat for a few minutes. Still nothing.

I climbed out of the chair and began poking around the parlor, picking things up, setting them down. There were some books. I'd dusted them enough. Since it was summer, I hadn't much looked at them. I walked up to the shelf . . . let's see . . . *A Tale of Two Cities* by Charles Dickens. I pulled it out and opened the book to the first chapter. "It was the best of times, it was the worst of times . . . ."

I kept reading through the paragraph. Dang, the whole first paragraph was one long sentence. Don't think so. I closed the book with a firm *whump*. No way was I going to read a book full of long sentences in the middle of the summer!

What else was there? *Oliver Twist*—I smiled at the title. Nice last name; it's got to be good. But when I glanced down at the author, my smile faded. Charles

Dickens—*him* again—fine, on to the next book. *Treasure Island* by Robert Lewis Stevenson. Treasure was promising. I pulled the book out and opened it to the first chapter and started reading. Nope, looked like a boy book. I put it back. *Little Women.* Definitely not a boy book, but was it a Lee book?

I hesitated before pulling it out. If I got caught reading *any* book, Lin and Will would tease me, but a book titled *Little Women* would downright ruin my reputation. I glanced around. *All clear.* I pulled out the book and opened it up. I started reading. After a few minutes I looked up with a start. *Wow, this was good,* I thought. I'd forgotten I was in the middle of the parlor, exposed for all to see. I tucked a finger between the pages to hold my spot and crept upstairs to my room.

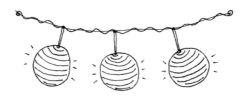

CHAPTER FOURTEEN

Saturday morning I was ready to nab Will just as soon as I saw him. I wanted to hear all about the big party. But when we finally crossed paths, I stopped short. He looked tired. His hair was more messed than usual, and his eyes were droopy. He was a pathetic-looking older brother. I was trying to decide whether or not to bother him when he saw me. To my surprised he perked up. "Hey, Lee, I've been looking for you. I gotta tell you about last night."

Fine by me! I thought. I followed him over to the front porch, and we sat down on the bottom step. Pork took up her spot between us. Before Will could say anything I had to ask, "Will, you look like death warmed over. What happened?"

"Yeah, well, I got home really late last night. Still, morning chores don't go away. Don't worry, I'll live—now let me tell you what happened."

His words began to tumble out. "There were three different bands playing and thousands of people. I heard one person say there were fourteen thousand guests. Mayor Snyder was there along with the City Council and a bunch of other officials. When Mr. Patterson came out, everyone cheered and waved their hankies. Men threw their hats into the air."

I couldn't help but wonder how the men all found the right hats later, once they were done throwing. I didn't ask, though, since Will was on a roll. I didn't want him to stop talking.

"Later on, everyone gathered under the trees. Tables covered with white tablecloths were lined up end to end, forming a huge oval. I was one of the servers who helped with the food. There must have been two hundred of us, all dressed in white coats. We served chicken and fish, all kinds of sandwiches, ice cream, cake, candy, and lemonade. We just kept handing out food and people kept eating.

"Then the cigars were passed out—twenty thousand cigars throughout the night were smoked, no kidding. Once everyone started puffing on their cigars there was so much smoke, it looked like the place was on fire. But it looked really pretty because the smoke caught the light from the lanterns. See, these big Japanese lanterns were strung throughout the woods, thousands of them, all red, green, yellow, and blue. The lights turned the smoke into colors."

I watched Will with amazement; he'd barely stopped to take a breath.

"Later on in the evening, Mr. Patterson showed

pictures from all over the world. After the picture show I helped clean up, but I could see the goings on. The bands played in different areas—did I tell you there were three different bands?"

I nodded.

"Yeah, well, and people were dancing, and the smoke and lanterns—you would have loved it. If Mr. Patterson ever throws another party, I'm going to try to get you in."

I looked closely at Will's face to see if he was pulling my leg, but he wasn't. He was serious. "Wow, Will, thanks, it would be really neat." I wanted to start quizzing him about when did he think there'd be another party, but instead I asked, "So'd you tell Mom?"

He just looked at me. "How do you think I got out of the house? She quizzed me. She wanted to know all about the picture show."

I thought about the pictures and briefly wondered if I wanted to know all about them—*nope*.

Just then we heard a ruckus at the end of the lane, and Pork got up to investigate. A few minutes later she trotted back, followed shortly by a bent little man—the knife sharpener, Mr. Jacobs. He was shorter than me and very thin. The only things big on him were his eyebrows and ears. His eyebrows stuck straight out and when he talked they seemed to dance. I always had to make an effort to keep from staring.

He brought his cart, filled with tools, up to the front of the house. He left it in the courtyard and then walked round to the summer kitchen. Will and I went back to our chores. The knife guy held no interest for us. He'd been stopping by every few months since we could remember, sharpening knives and tools for a fee.

After a bit, I decided to check and see if my mother had any cookies that needed sampling. I entered the summer kitchen as Mr. Jacobs was leaving. Just after I sat down with a hot cookie the door burst open. It was Mr. Jacobs. His eyes were wide, and his eyebrows quivered as he began to stammer, "I didn't see . . . the cat . . . I'm so sorry . . . ."

My mother said, "Now, hold on Mr. Jacobs, what's wrong?"

He took a deep breath. "I believe I just ran over one of your cats."

My heart sank and I forgot about the cookie.

My mother took a deep breath and asked, "Mr. Jacobs, is the cat alive?"

When he nodded, she narrowed her eyes and asked, "Was it a grey kitten?"

"Why, yes. Yes, it was a grey kitten, but . . . ."

"It's okay, Mr. Jacobs, it wasn't your fault; it's just that kitten."

He looked at her blankly and she went on. "I don't know how to explain it," she said, "but he's probably fine. Where is he?"

"He ran off after I, well, you know."

"Are you sure you ran him over?"

"Oh, yes," he nodded enthusiastically. "There was a thunk and a loud screech, and so I turned around and looked and saw a grey streak running across the yard into the barn, and—"

"Okay, well, why don't we go look for him?"

Mr. Jacobs and I followed my mother as she calmly led the way to the barn. I was more numb than upset. We had already been through so much with Eutychus that this just seemed to fit.

Inside the barn, we found the kitten huddled in a corner. My mother picked him up gently and he squeaked in pain. Peering over her shoulder, I could see that his back leg was broken.

Now I was upset. "Oh, Mom . . . ."

"Shhh, it'll be all right. Mr. Jacobs, please don't worry yourself anymore. I'm sure you need to be on your way, and we don't want to keep you. Thank you for your concern."

She smiled at the poor man as he nodded and backed out of the barn.

My mother walked back into the house holding the kitten. By this time Annie, Jasper, and Will had joined us, and we all trailed behind her. We went into the kitchen and sat down. She put the kitten on the table and it tried to stand but couldn't. A tear made its way down my cheek.

"Is he going to die?" I asked.

Mother was quiet while she continued to examine him. After a few minutes, she sat back.

"It doesn't look like anything besides the leg was damaged. But the leg is broken in three places. We can try to splint it."

A quick search of the house produced a few sticks and wraps, but we couldn't figure out how to keep everything in place. The kitten was surprisingly accommodating. He would lie there while we fussed and tied. Once we were finished, he wriggled a bit and shed the bandages, then settled back while we tried again.

Finally, my mother said, "This isn't going to work, but I do have an idea. When I was a little girl we had a cat that got in a scuffle with a coyote. He ended up with a broken leg. Your grandfather had me put him in a box and we kept him quiet. After about a month, the cat was as good as new. Cats will heal if you leave them alone. What if we do that with Eutychus?"

We had nothing to lose. The only other option was one I didn't want to think about. I found a box and put a soft cloth in the bottom. Two small cups for water and food followed, and then we put Eutychus in his new home. As I looked at him I thought, *More prayer was definitely in order.* The box was put in the kitchen next to the stove, and my mother promised that she'd watch over him. Now all we needed to do was wait for him to heal.

CHAPTER FIFTEEN

The next Friday, Will came home from work just before supper. When I said 'Hi,' he just groaned in my direction.

"What's wrong?" I asked.

"Got a belly ache," he grumbled and made his way up to his room.

He made it down to supper looking a bit better. Still, he just picked at his food.

"Will, what's wrong with you?" my mother asked. "You love stew."

"It's good, mom, I just ate a whole bunch of ice cream today."

I glared at him. I couldn't believe I was worried about him.

"I got to help out with a party Mr. Patterson put on for the Dayton children," Will said. "Man, there were tons of kids everywhere. I mean, they behaved and all, but it's a lot of work scooping up all that ice cream."

Utilizing all of my self-control, I held my tongue. At least I tried, but it didn't work, "I thought you were going to try and get me in to help with the next party," I said.

Will grimaced in my direction. "I was, I mean, I am. I just—I didn't know about today. During work I was asked to help out. They had more kids show up than they expected. Two thousand children. Do you have any idea what two thousand children look like?" he asked with a groan. Then he smiled, "Who'd have thought kids would come out of the woodwork for ice cream?" His face fell and he sighed.

My father looked at Will and said, "There's more, isn't there." He wasn't asking, he *knew*.

Will's shoulders slumped. "I found out this afternoon that Mr. King, Joe's dad, was fired because of that Palmer guy."

"Did he do something wrong?"

"No, that's just it. Mr. King loved NCR and worked really hard. He just asked the wrong question, and before we knew it he was fired."

"What do you mean the wrong question?"

"He questioned the need for horseback riding. Mr. Palmer had started a riding program for the executives and it wasn't very popular. Some people have even been hurt. Mr. King asked if anything else could be made available for those who didn't feel comfortable around horses.

"Mr. Palmer just looked at him and said that his question showed 'an appalling lack of character' and walked away. Two days later, Mr. King got fired. It's just not fair."

"You won't be working for a few weeks, right?" Dad knew that the factory closed the first two weeks of August for vacation. This had been Will's last workday before the factory shut down. "Why don't you take the time to think things over and decide if you want to stay?"

"I like the factory. I haven't soured on it. I just don't like Mr. Palmer."

"Just the same, take the time to cool your heels a bit, okay?" Then my father changed the subject. "Hey, Lee, what have you been up to?"

"Oh, nothing much."

"Come on, Lee, you've been up to something. What were you doing in your room all afternoon?" my mother asked.

"Reading," I said as nonchalantly as possible. Everyone started laughing, thinking I was kidding. My glare told them otherwise and the laughter died down.

"Really?" she asked.

"Yeah, I've really been reading." Desperately I tried to change the subject. "What about Lin, what have you been up to? Are the brothers ready to fly yet?"

"No," said Lin, for once not interested in flight.

"What have you been reading?"

Everyone waited. I couldn't believe this was coming up at dinner, I was trapped. "Lillwmn," I mumbled.

"What?" He prodded.

"Lillwmn," I said with a bit more force, desperately trying to think of another subject.

"Come on Lee, give us a break," Will chimed in.

"She's been reading *Little Women*, I saw her," volunteered Jasper. I glared at him and thought, *Oh go wipe your nose.* Leave it up to the little squirt to turn me in, and leave it up to him to notice. I'd begun to realize that there was a lot more to this six-year-old than any of us gave him credit for. Jasper could move around without any of us taking much notice. I saw now that he was utilizing the situation to his advantage. I decided to start watching him more closely.

Will and Lin snickered behind their hands. Annie looked at me with newfound respect. My mother smiled and said, "That was my book when I was your age; it had just come out. I love the story. Good for you, Lee. Okay, everyone, time to clean up."

With that, my torture was over.

CHAPTER SIXTEEN

The next two weeks I had Will for company. It was great. A few days we went and visited Lin and the Wright brothers out at Huffman field. The plane was coming together well. Surprisingly, they had taken my rather grumpy suggestion seriously and made the front piece—what they call the elevator—bigger. They seemed to think the change would help them steer better.

August in Dayton was very humid. Everything looked faded, and everyone moved like they were going through water—which was nearly true. Every time we visited the barn it was much too hot. It felt like an oven, although none of the men seemed to pay attention to the heat. The Wright brothers still wore their wool suits and somehow managed to keep clean, in spite of all the work they were doing. Lin had caught the flying bug and was happy to help out in whatever way he could. He didn't care if he cooked in the process. Will and

I never stayed long. It was too hot, too sticky, and too much work for us.

On one of our trips I found out they'd been working at flying for a while. "The first time we really flew was in 1903, at Kitty Hawk, North Carolina," Orville explained. "We really didn't know what we were doing, but we were in the air. We're hoping that this airplane, we call it the Wright Flyer III, will be the first practical airplane. We proved that flight is possible, now we're taking the next step. We're figuring out *how* to fly."

Wilber chimed in. "You see, moving through the air involves a number of factors. It's not like moving an object along the ground; there you're only dealing with forward motion. In the air there's not only forward motion but up, down, side to side, and air currents thrown in just to keep things interesting. There's much less room for error in the air. Sudden stops are not good."

After Wilber's explanation Orville smiled and said, "We're making headway. With our launching derrick we've been able to spend more time in the sky. Before we built the launch derrick we had to lay track every time we wanted to fly. We set it according to the direction of the wind, and I don't want to tell you how many times we were all set to go and the wind changed! With the weight and pulley system we can leave the track in place. That saves so much time in the preparation and we have more time in the air."

He looked at the other two men with a nod. "Now we're doing it, we're really doing it. We even want to carry a passenger someday." He smiled at me. "It's been something," he said. I smiled back and didn't say a word. I didn't see how flying could ever be something practical, but then again, I never thought a person could fly. Underestimating the Wright brothers seemed like a bad idea.

One day, heading home from the field, Will began to hatch a plan. After Mr. King got fired I had groused that someone needed to teach Mr. Palmer a lesson. Someone should stand up to him and give him a good swift kick in the pants. Usually Will doesn't pay much mind to what I say, but this time it stuck in his noggin.

He got a determined look and said, "We've got to come up with a plan, Lee. You can help out. We need to teach Mr. Palmer a lesson."

"What do you mean a lesson? I wasn't real serious about that, you know." I didn't like the direction Will was heading. "You don't want to hurt him, do you?"

"Dang, Lee, don't get all nervous. Of course not! I just want to play a few practical jokes on him. Maybe get him to take himself less seriously, or at least it'll get his attention off firing folks."

Well, that seemed a bit more noble than just being plain mean. And so the rest the time Will had off, we worked on a plan. Lin helped out, too, offering suggestions here and there. Just before Will was due back to work the plan was completed, perfect in its simplicity and deviousness. We were all quite pleased with ourselves. It'd be great, especially if we didn't end up getting skinned alive.

CHAPTER SEVENTEEN

When the big day came I woke up decidedly uneasy, wondering how in the heck I'd gotten roped into such nonsense, but there was no turning back.

Will went into work a bit early and stashed a big bag of goodies in a janitor's closet close by Palmer's office. A few hours later, I headed in, dressed up just like Will. I was sporting his hat, jacket, and old pants. I walked onto the NCR grounds like I knew what I was doing, just stealing glances at the map Will drew for me once in a while.

It was everything I could do not to stumble around gaping at the place. The complex was huge, bigger than I had expected, and really pretty. The buildings were made of brick with big windows looking out on the grounds, which were landscaped with wide lawns and flowers. It didn't look like a factory.

I almost got lost a few times, but finally located the right building. I headed in a side door, up a flight of stairs, down a hallway, and finally was able to duck into the same janitor's closet occupied by Will's bag. I could have stayed there the rest of the day, and I would have been happy as a clam. As it was, I was terrified. All this was way over my head.

I turned a bucket upside down, sat down on it, and waited. The waiting didn't help. The longer I sat the more nervous I became. It was all I could do to stay still, but the closet was dark and I didn't want to bump into anything. When Will finally opened the door, I almost passed out. I jumped, and he frowned and shushed me. *Creep!* I thought. Here I was doing this for him, and he has the nerve to shush me.

"Come on," he said, "it's 10:30. Mr. Palmer just left for his meeting." Every day Mr. Palmer met with all the department heads and taught them new and unusual ways to exercise their bodies. In turn, they were supposed to go share their newfound enlightenment with their underlings. We had an hour.

The hallway was empty. Most everyone who had offices on this floor was also part of the Palmer meeting. We walked up to the door of his office. Will put his hand on the doorknob and turned. For a moment I thought my prayers had been answered and the door was locked. It wasn't to be. Much to my dismay, the door opened. Before us, the office waited.

My stomach flip-flopped as we started to work. We had planned on moving his file drawers around, but they were too heavy. Instead, Will and I handed folders back and forth, thoroughly shuffling the information. After that, Will went to work lightly drizzling honey in Mr. Palmer's hat and then moved on to his jacket, sewing the arms closed about halfway down. I focused on Mr. Palmer's desk.

By now I'd settled into the task. I put my heart into switching the desk's contents from drawer to drawer. Mr. Palmer now had his paperclips in the bottom drawer next to his comic books. I took a small flask he had hidden in his desk and stuck it in the top drawer of his file cabinet. Then I used some soap from Will's bag of tricks and slicked up the drawers so that they were easy to open. I topped each drawer off with feathers and then lightly glued most of the doors shut—just so he'd have to pull extra hard to get them moving. I wedged open the middle drawer, now full of sawdust (also from the bag), just a bit—so he'd have to tug. Satisfied with my work, I looked up to tell Will what I'd done, but he was no longer in the room.

Sakes alive! I'd been so intent on the task that I didn't know he'd left. I began to panic. I sat at the desk and tried to slow down my breathing and the pounding in my head. *Think, think,* I said to myself. *Think, breathe, think.*

Gingerly, I crept to the door and peeked out. Nothing, no one—all was quiet. I looked out the window. No one was around outside. I tried to think of what I should do, but my brain didn't want to work.

Then I heard a weird sound. It was a clomping,

and it was getting closer. I crouched to the side of the door and held my breath. The sound was really close now. Suddenly the door flung open, and a smiling Will poked his head through the door, his finger to his lips. He walked into the office leading a horse. It seemed Will had someone else in on the whole project. He got the horse all the way into the office and handed the lead rope to me. He was out of breath but managed to gasp, "Keep her quiet," and then turned around to leave.

I grabbed him. "No, I'm not staying here with this horse."

"You've got to. I have one more thing I want to get."

"You left me! I didn't know where you were—you scared the daylights out of me."

He grinned. "I wanted to surprise you. Did it work?"

I opened my mouth to say something, but could only manage a squeak, so I punched him. He laughed and headed out the door. The horse and I looked at each other. I had nothing to say, but the horse shook her head and nickered as if to say, "How did we end up in the middle of this?" And then, as if to make her point, she lifted her tail and relieved herself. *Unbelievable*, I thought. Whew. My eyes started to burn and I was getting lightheaded from trying to hold my breath. Finally, I opened up a window. I figured that'd be better than me passing out, and

Will having to haul me out by a leg or something.

In the meantime, Will went down the hall, turned a corner, ran down the stairs—and right into Mr. Palmer. It seemed that Mr. Palmer's meetings didn't always last an hour. So Will turned and followed Mr. Palmer back up the stairs, trying desperately to slow him down and somehow warn me.

Will babbled on about how interested he was in exercise and getting healthy. Mr. Palmer kept walking, grunting from time to time as if to show he cared. Once the two entered the hallway that led to Palmer's office, Will stopped and said rather loudly, "Man alive, MR. PALMER, I didn't know that YOUR OFFICE was on this floor. Well, shucks, I thought you worked on the other side of the factory. Well, I'll be SKEDADDLING now. Bye, thanks for talking to me."

Through Will's final monologue, Palmer stared at Will, quite possibly wondering if he'd been dropped on his head at a tender age. With a final wave, Will ducked down the hall and hightailed it out of the building.

In the office I had heard Will's "Mr. Palmer," and desperately began looking around. This was not how things were supposed to go. I couldn't sneak out the door. I was stuck in a booby-trapped office with a horse and its contribution. I heard "Skedaddle, Bye" from Will and knew that it was only a matter of seconds before my young life would end. Then I spied the open window. Just before I climbed out the window I noticed my sack, grabbed it, and then slipped out the window onto a small ledge. To the left of the ledge was a drainpipe. I grabbed it and shimmied down. As my feet touched the ground, I heard Mr. Palmer enter his office. I could tell because he started yelling, and the horse started clumping around in earnest.

But I was safe. Then I realized that I was standing in front of one of the big, ground-floor windows. Even worse, there was a man standing on the other side of the glass looking at me. As we looked at each other, Palmer—above me—started to swear. He seemed to have a knack for it.

The man on the other side of the window pointed at me and crooked his finger as if to say "Come here." I looked for a way to escape. He shook his head and once again crooked his finger. I was stuck, and I knew that any second Mr. Palmer was going to stick his head out his window.

Since the man looked pretty harmless—glasses, kind eyes, young and mild mannered—I went in the side door. He met me at the door, shutting it behind me. I looked around at the big office, separated from other offices by half-walls and glass partitions. Several men around the room were tinkering on different pieces of cash registers. While I looked over the room the man looked me over and then said, "Boy, you work here?"

"No, sir." I briefly thought about correcting him concerning my gender, but I was in enough trouble already. Time to tread lightly and smile.

"You do now. Grab a broom."

I couldn't say no, so I grabbed a broom and started sweeping. I tried to ignore the thumping from above. A few minutes later, Mr. Palmer burst through his door and asked if anyone had seen someone come out of his office. He was a mess. It looked like he'd had a close encounter with the horse. There were also feathers in his hair and sawdust sticking to the front of his shirt. I was torn between holding back a smile and running in terror.

The man who had just given me my new job looked at him and said, "Now, Charles, how could we see anyone leave your office? It's above us." Mr. Palmer sputtered and stormed out. I kept sweeping.

We were all quiet for a moment. The man turned to me and said, "Son, is there a horse upstairs?" The men around the room chuckled.

I didn't look up and just kept sweeping, "Yes, sir."

"I'm assuming that you had something to do with that."

"Um, yes, sir."

"You've been busy. Let's see how hard you can work here. Two times a week, sweep up and keep things from getting dusty, but don't throw anything out. What's your name?"

I couldn't believe my ears. He was offering me a job!

I managed to gasp, "My name's Lee, sir." I knew I should just leave well enough alone, but I couldn't. "Uh, if you know I caused all that trouble, how come you're hiring me?"

More chuckles erupted from around the room. "With you around, it won't be boring here, that's for sure." He laughed and slapped me on the back, "You can call me Boss Ket."

My eyes flew wide open, even though I tried not to seem surprised. I'd heard about Boss Ket— Charles Kettering. Will couldn't stop talking about him, because he was a real live inventor. From Will's description I would have thought he wouldn't be so normal looking.

I must have looked thunderstruck, because Boss Ket asked "You okay, Lee? What's wrong?"

"Yes, sir, I was just thinking your insides don't much match your outside."

"What's that, son?"

"Well, I've heard about you and I thought you'd be . . . bigger."

Boss Ket just laughed and said, "Keep sweeping, Lee."

CHAPTER EIGHTEEN

When I got home mid-afternoon, Will and Lin were waiting for me. Will was home early—he'd told his boss he was sick. Guess he couldn't stand not knowing what happened to me. As soon as I walked up the lane, Will and Lin pelted me with questions.

I didn't answer right off. Instead, I walked for a bit, sighed, and managed to look sad and distressed. I try to never miss the chance to make the boys squirm, and this was a great opportunity. I kept them waiting till they looked ready to burst, then I gave them the details.

When I mentioned the horse and what it did as soon as Will left the office, Lin interrupted me. "Horse, what horse? Nothing was ever mentioned about a horse when we were planning all this. Where did the horse come from?"

"Yeah, Will," I added. "I've been wondering the same thing."

Will explained, "I mentioned to Joe King what we

were planning and he came up with the idea of a horse. Mr. Patterson's farm is right next to the factory and he arranged to slip a horse out in such a way that everyone at the stable could claim ignorance. No one got into trouble. Then we figured out a route to move the horse from the farm to the office. By following the train tracks most of the way, there were less windows for people to see what we were up to. I met Joe by the door of Mr. Palmer's building and brought the horse up the stairs to the office. No big deal. So, Lee, what happened next?"

I stared at Will thinking, *No big deal? Leave it to Will to figure out how to sneak a horse through NCR without anyone noticing.* "I heard you outside the office with Mr. Palmer. You really saved me with that one. Can you imagine if you hadn't gone back out? We'd *both* be strung up."

Judging from Will's pale face I guess he hadn't thought about that. I told them about shimmying down the drainpipe just before Mr. Palmer walked into his office.

"Wow, you got away clean. That's great," said Will.

"No, I didn't."

"What?" they both exclaimed.

"No, I didn't get away clean. Once I got down, I realized that a man saw my whole escape. He was standing at the ground floor window watching me."

"Who was he? Did he turn you in? Was he mad?" Will asked.

"No," I said casually, then added, "He had me come inside then gave me a job."

"What!" they both shouted.

"Do you guys practice this or what? Yeah, he told me to get a broom and start sweeping. You know, he really saved me because I don't think I would have gotten away otherwise. If I'd run off, Mr. Palmer would have seen me. Someone would have noticed me if I'd tried sneaking around the building. As it was, a few minutes after I got there, Mr. Palmer came through the office looking for me. All the folks in the office acted like nothing was up. It was great."

"Unbelievable! How'd Mr. Palmer look?" Will asked.

I grinned. "He looked pretty rough. He'd stepped into the horse poop, had it part way up his pant leg. There were feathers in his hair, too. He must have tried to open up one of my booby-trapped drawers. You know, I felt kinda sorry for him—he looked really rattled."

"Yeah, well, you notice that no one came running to his aid, right?"

I thought about it for a moment. "You know, you're right. Everyone had a good laugh when he left. He must have made a whole bunch of people mad in the short time he's been at the factory."

"Sounds like it," Lin agreed. "So, who was the guy in the window?"

I couldn't help but smile. "Well, let me see, I

think he told me to call him . . . now what was it? Oh, yeah, Boss Ket."

The silence that followed was really quite gratifying. I'd graduated from "What" into silent astonishment.

"Boss Ket gave you a job," Will finally said. "Aren't you something else?"

"Yeah, twice a week I go sweep up," I said, trying my best not to gloat. "He said I'd keep things interesting."

"He has no idea," said Lin with a laugh. "Come on, we have to figure out how to tell Mom and Dad you have a job."

CHAPTER NINETEEN

My job was almost short-lived. My second day at NCR Mr. Patterson himself, with a long trail of visitors, came through. Apparently he was showing off his factory but was not pleased by the level of disarray he encountered at Inventions Department #3. He pulled up short and then stormed out, calling the place an "untidy mess." A short time later a messenger arrived with a note that informed Mr. Kettering that he was fired. If he left, I didn't have a job. Besides, it was just wrong.

"What—fired?" I sputtered. "He can't fire you!"

Much to my surprise my comment was met by laughter. "Well, he *can* fire me, Lee," explained Boss Ket. He grinned. "In fact, he's fired me before. Fortunately, Mr. Patterson lacks a perfect memory." Then Will arrived, delivering another message, from Edward Deeds, one of the top brass at the factory. He was the man who had hired Charles Kettering a year before. Boss Ket took the note from Will and thanked him. He read the note, smiled, and held it up. "Well, boys, it looks like I've been hired back!"

The next day frosted glass panels were installed where clear panes had been before. This was by special request from Mr. Patterson. He never wanted visitors to see the Inventions Department #3 again.

Working in the department was great, but I wasn't there for long stretches of time. The place was pretty small, so it took more time for me to travel to the factory than it took me to sweep. But it was worth the trip. I loved watching Boss Ket and his crew in action. They all worked together on projects. They'd talk through a problem and bounce ideas off each other. If the problem started to get too big in people's minds, Boss Ket would say, "There are no unsolvable problems, just problems that we don't know how to solve." He really believed it.

One day he told me, "Lee, always remember that anything a man can imagine, he can do, provided he does what nature wants him to. The only problem is to find out how to do it." Then he asked me if I had any ideas about a project he was working on. I stammered out a few suggestions, and he listened patiently. He said, "See, there're a whole lot of things going on in your mind. Make sure and share 'em. You've got a great deal to offer."

A few days later Boss Ket asked Bill Chryst, one of the men in the department, about "the boys from

Kitty Hawk." Of course, I was all ears. He wanted to know if Bill had ever heard of them and if he knew about them trying to fly. When Bill said he'd known them for years, and they were flying like mad just east of town, Boss Ket asked, "Could you arrange it so that I could meet them sometime? I'd really like that."

Just then someone behind them grumbled, "Sounds like swamp people to me."

"What?" asked Bill.

"You know, a bunch of nonsense, like the swamp people. Remember earlier this summer when there were all those reports about swamp monsters? It was in the paper. They called them swamp people. For weeks rumors flew about swamp people and how dangerous they were. Everyone was saying they saw 'em here and saw 'em there. But nothing ever came of it. Never heard such a bunch of balderdash. I think these flying brothers are more of the same."

I thought back to the Saturday Lin, Will, and I spent playing in the mud, and I squeaked. I didn't mean to, it just came out. The men stopped talking and looked at me. I tried to look nonchalant, but my brain was spinning. There was no way it could have anything to do with the boys and me. No way.

"What was that, Lee?" Bill asked.

"Oh, well, I hadn't heard about the swamp people. When did people see them?"

Someone said the end of May, and I started to

relax—good, it wasn't the boys and me. But then he was corrected by another man, "No, I remember, it was during all that rain in June, and it was a Saturday, I'm sure of it. One of the folks who claimed to see them was heading to town for a Saturday visit."

"That's right," someone else chimed in, "He's right, I remember now."

I must have looked a bit pale because Boss Ket looked at me and smiled, "Relax, Lee, there're no swamp monsters running around terrorizing folks. At least, I'm pretty sure you'll never run into one."

The men laughed and went back to their tasks.

Holy cow, my father was right, people *did* take notice. I didn't know if I should laugh or beg forgiveness. I did know that keeping my mouth shut right now was a really good idea. I just kept sweeping.

CHAPTER TWENTY

That night at supper, Lin announced that the Wright brothers planned on trying out their new airplane design the next day. Since it was Wednesday, and neither Will nor I worked on Wednesday, we could both go out and watch with Lin. We'd get to see the Wright Flyer III's first flight.

After supper, I pulled Will and Lin aside and told them about the swamp people. Lin had a good laugh, and Will started figuring out how we could do it again and whom we could scare.

I dug my heels in on this one. "No way, Will. We got away with this once. I'm not doing that again. Besides, that mud was itchy."

Mention of the itch pretty well soured Will on the project. But we figured we'd visit the library and look up the story about the swamp monsters. At least we'd get to see what trouble we stirred up. For the rest of the night we entertained each other by making swamp monster faces. Mom caught us once and just shook her head. "Strange children, so very strange," she lamented.

But then she got serious. "Lee, I have to talk with you about that kitten. He's driving me nuts." The kitten had been steadily getting better. His leg was mending, and he was getting more adventurous.

"What's he doing?"

"Everything. That stupid cat keeps trying to jump in the spring barrel. He'd drown, you know, if he ever gets in there and I'm not around to fish him out. He's been jumping on the top of the stove, and it's hot. He seems to find every dangerous thing there is in the kitchen and then carries on with it."

"I thought he was in his box."

"Oh, lordy, no, that only lasted for about a week. Then he started trying to get out. That was awful enough because his leg wasn't cooperating, but once his leg started to firm up, he began getting out of the box in earnest. Now I'm pulling out my hair."

My mother looked frazzled. She *never* looked frazzled. I knew what needed to be done. "Mom, when the Gypsies gave me the kitty, they said I'd know when it was time to give him up. I can't take the excitement anymore. This is nuts."

"Amen, Lee. I was hoping you'd say that. Let's give him another week or so to heal up a bit more. Meanwhile we can figure out what to do with him. We need to find someone willing to take him."

Will started to laugh. "I've got a great idea. I know the perfect person."

"Who?" My mother asked.

"Palmer, Mr. Palmer."

I shook my head. "Why would he be willing to take a kitten, and how could we give it to him? What do you want me to do," I asked, "march up to his office and say, here's a crazy kitty. By the way, how'd you like the horse?"

"No, but there is a big cotillion next week, Friday night—I was going to tell you about it—Mr. Palmer will be there for sure. If a sweet little girl, dressed up in a pretty party dress and a big bow in her hair came up to him at the dance with a basket and presented him with the gift of a kitten, I bet he couldn't resist."

"Who'd we get to do that?" I asked.

"You."

Now it was my mother's turn to start laughing. "You know it's just not right to do to the man, no matter how ornery he is, but I'd be willing to go along with the whole thing just to see Leah dressed up like that."

"Mom!"

"Well, I would, Lee. You know, it just might work. From what I've heard, Mr. Palmer lives alone in town, and that's what Eutychus needs—a nice, safe, inside home. Maybe it will work out, the kitten will be safe and Mr. Palmer will have some company . . . and some excitement."

I just smiled. This was going to be worse than messing with Mr. Palmer's office. The plan involved a dress.

Mom frowned. "We should tell the Gypsies. I'll make apple pie tomorrow."

None of us questioned the statement. We all knew that if mom made apple pie, Mr. and Mrs. Stanley, the Gypsies, would visit. But I had an idea about how they managed to show up like they did.

Early the next morning, I went outside and took my post high up in an oak tree. I stayed until it was time for breakfast. After breakfast I ran back and resumed my lookout. Chores would have to wait.

I just settled in when Jasper crept around the side of the house. He looked around to see if anyone was watching, paused to swipe his nose, and then he headed down the lane.

Once he was out of sight, I climbed down from the tree and headed after him. Once Jasper got to the main road he took out a red hankie and tied it to a tree limb that stuck out into the road. I ducked behind a tree just as he turned, swiped his nose, and trotted back up the road towards the house.

Sure enough, early afternoon the Gypsies came by. They talked with mom, laughing as she recount-ed the exploits of the kitten. Mr. Stanley said that he didn't know the kitten would be so much trouble, but he'd been a bit different since he was born. He also said that we were good to keep him for so long, but it might be time to find him a new home. We agreed with him and said we were working on doing just that.

As they climbed back into their wagon, Mr. Stanley, with a wink and a smile, tossed Jasper a piece of gum. Jasper smiled back. We waved goodbye, and a few minutes later I hotfooted it down the lane. When I got to the road, the kerchief was still there. I untied it, brought it to the house.

Just after I returned, Jasper came out from the barn and trotted down the lane. When he was out of sight, I took out his hankie and tied it around my head. Then I lounged on the front porch step with Pork. A few minutes later he returned looking confused and worried. When he saw me he stopped, swiped, and then came over and sat down beside me on the porch. We sat there for a while saying nothing, and he finally said, "So, are you going to tell anyone?"

"Heck, no, I wouldn't want to mess up your arrangement. Besides, it's fun watching everyone try to puzzle out how the Gypsies always show up. I just finally figured out they had to have help—you."

"Yeah, I think I was four when we started doing this. I was playing in the lane by myself, and they stopped and talked with me on their way up to the house. I mentioned that mom was making apple pie, and, well, it just built from there."

"I bet you'll keep the boys going for years."

Jasper looked at me and smiled. "I've kept *you* going for years," he said.

He had a point.

CHAPTER TWENTY-ONE

The next day Lin, Will, and I did our chores as fast as possible. Once we were finished, we headed off to Huffman Prairie. By the time we got there, the Wright brothers and Charlie were already hard at work. They had the plane assembled and loaded on the launch derrick. It was exciting to walk up to the barn, rather than hide in the woods.

When we got there, Wilbur frowned at the three of us. "Now, you all must be in a safe place while this gets off the ground. Maybe you should stand over in the barn."

"Yes, sir," we answered and headed towards the barn. We'd figured it was all right to show up and watch since Lin had been helping out. Maybe we should have asked. I looked at Lin, knowing he was a bit disappointed about being stuck in the barn after working with the men. But just as we got to the barn, Wilbur called out, "Hey, Lin, can you give us a hand over here for a minute?"

Lin brightened up and trotted over to the men.

Will and I sat around for the next half hour or so. Then we started to poke around, fiddling with the tools in the barn. We were back to sitting when Lin finally burst in, shouting, "It's time!"

We could see the end of the derrick from the door of the barn and strained to catch the first glimpse. We heard the engine sputter, then catch and go. We heard the rumble of the weight dropping, and the plane shot by like greased lightning.

I braced myself, remembering what happened the last time Orville flew. This time Wilbur was flying, but I wasn't sure what to expect. The plane rose in the air, gently dipped its wing, and turned left. It straightened out and continued down the field paralleling the tree line. Again it turned left, and again.

Suddenly it was heading right towards us, and past, rounding the field for another loop. It made a circle, and it was still going. I sat down in the front of the barn and watched the sight. After a few loops the plane wobbled a bit too much, but then steadied and landed. Orville and Charlie ran out to the plane smiling. The three of us kids whooped and jumped out. All of us worked to lug the plane back to the derrick.

As we lugged, I asked Orville how much the plane weighed. He said about 700 pounds. Since he didn't seem to mind my questions, I asked him how much the big weight on the "launch derrick" weighed. He said it weighed 1,600 pounds.

Dang! I thought, *No wonder it worked so well.*

We watched them set up and make two more flights, each longer than the last. I began to notice a few details of how they flew the airplane, and Lin pointed out what he knew. They seemed to be using two levers for control. Lin said that there was a hip thing they used by shifting their weight that helped them turn. It was so amazing to think that they could control such a big machine as it made its way through the air.

Finally, I nudged Lin. "We'd better be heading home. We need to give Dad a hand bringing in the hay before supper."

"Yeah, you're right," he said. We thanked the men for letting us watch and began our long walk home. As usual, we talked over what we saw. We had seen the Wright brothers go beyond quick jumps. Now they were flying in earnest.

CHAPTER TWENTY-TWO

The next day, at the Inventions Department #3, I was in for an unpleasant surprise. When I arrived, everyone was talking and upset. Word arrived that Boss Ket had taken a nasty fall off a horse, and no one knew how he was doing. I tried to sweep, but like everyone else I eventually gave up and waited.

An hour later, Boss Ket himself limped in the door. Everyone started asking questions at once. "Hold on," he said, "Hold on and I'll tell you all about it." Bill brought him a chair and he sat down.

"You all know how Mr. Patterson has taken to doing reviews on horseback, right? Well, he got all the factory's executives lined up on horses in this big field. When he gave the signal, we were supposed to ride our horses down the field, one at a time, with great skill and agility. But my horse didn't see things that way." Everyone started laughing.

Bill asked, "You're not talking about that big,

mean-looking horse they tried to get you on a few weeks ago."

"That's Midnight to you, sir. And, yes, I am. That horse hates me. I don't know why, but he does. So, it comes up my turn and I gave him a little kick so he'd canter. Well, he laid his ears back and started running down the field full out. Then the evil beast proved his timing was impeccable. He came to a full stop right in front of Mr. Patterson. I, on the other hand, did not. Instead of continuing to sit regally on my noble steed, I shot right over Midnight's head and landed square at the feet of my employer's well-mannered mount. Or should I say, former employer."

"Oh, no," someone ribbed, "you got fired again. You should start keeping track, you might be setting some kind of record."

"Yeah, well, I guess I didn't make the most noble picture crumpled up into a heap. Edward Deeds was right next to him. Once he realized I was still in one piece he almost fell off his own horse trying not to laugh. But I know he'll take care of everything. On the bright side, I'm thinking this gets me out of the horse business for now. Don't worry, I'm fine, just a bit bruised."

It was time for all of us to get back to work, so I picked up my broom and started sweeping. I watched the men as I moved around the room. Some of them worked at a drawing board, while others worked on old cash registers or new ones. Bill Chryst was fiddling with a part and sifting through a box of nuts, bolts, springs, and wires, looking for something to catch his fancy.

I moved over to him. "What'cha looking for?" I asked.

"A spring," he said, "'bout an inch long, but thick."

I dug into my pocket—nope—and tried another pocket. Then I pulled out a spring, removed some lint, and held it out to him.

"How about this one, Mr. Chryst?"

He smiled and took the spring from my fingers. "Thanks, Lee, it's perfect. Where did you get this?"

"Since I started working here, I began collecting odds and ends I've come across lying around. That was one of 'em."

"Great job, young man!"

I just smiled. Someday I'd have to break the truth to them about this young man stuff.

CHAPTER TWENTY-THREE

I don't know why a body has to spend so much time primping for a stupid party, but that's what I had to do. My mother fussed over me, curling what little hair I had, then pinning it up with bows. If I hadn't been on such an important undertaking, I would have never agreed to all the nonsense.

My mother knew there was no turning back for me, and she was enjoying herself. We pulled out my Sunday clothes and polished my shoes. The dress was so clean and perfect I felt like a fool. It would all be over soon, I promised myself. My mother gave me a basket with a handle, and we put a big white bow on it and a soft cloth on the inside. I placed Eutychus inside and pulled the cloth over him.

Eutychus' leg had healed nicely. The timing for the party turned out to be a window of opportunity—Eutychus was between major catastrophes. Looking back, there weren't many times the kitten had been in one piece since we got him. Now that Eutychus was up and around, he was already at it again. The day before, he had gotten out of his box, out of the kitchen, and into the horse pasture. Once there, he headed for the closest horse, Daisy, and began playing with her tail.

Mother called Will to come help her, all the while muttering about how that animal was piling on the agony for her. She had Will lead the horse away from the kitten so that she could scoop up the kitten without being kicked. She held the kitten up in front of her. "Don't you know that horses kick?" she asked. The kitten just purred at her.

Tonight, the kitten was content to stay in the basket. He seemed to know that it was time to move on. Will was already at the cotillion, serving food. He had arranged to meet me by the road about halfway through the evening. My father joined in the project and gave me a ride in our buggy. When we got to the dance I was so amazed at the sight I almost forgot the cat.

There were lanterns strung through the trees, just like Will had described. The lanterns were rose, gold, green, and violet. A dance platform to the south had rose lanterns stacked high in a pyramid. I kissed my father good-bye, and he promised to be back in an hour. I headed off to find Will.

Will wasn't where he said he'd be, so I started walking towards the crowd. Just before I reached the edge, Will slipped up by my side. "Sorry about that.

I had to help mix some lemonade." Then, tender brother that he was, Will grabbed my hand just to show me how sticky his hands were from mixing the lemonade.

"Great. Thanks, Will, that was nice." Then I sighed, "Well, I'd better get to it. Have you seen Mr. Palmer?"

Will pointed me in the direction he'd last seen Mr. Palmer. It was so odd to walk across the grounds. There were people I'd seen around the factory, but none of them knew who I was. Tonight I was a young lady. I had to fight not to start laughing. About halfway across the grass a kind voice stopped me, "What do you have in your basket, miss?"

I knew that voice; it belonged to Boss Ket. No way was I going to turn around. I kept walking and said over my shoulder in my highest voice, "Oh, it's a present, a kitten."

"A kitten? Can I see?"

No, no, no you can't, I almost said, but then I thought, no one else has recognized me, *why should he?* I decided to remain calm. I stopped and turned, smiling sweetly, "Why, yes, of course you can."

His smile faltered a bit when he looked at me, and then he looked down as I pulled back the napkin. There lay Eutychus. I scooped out the kitten and held him up. Boss Ket made the appropriate approving noises and scratched his ears. Then I put the kitten back in the basket. As I removed my hand, fur stuck to the lemonade slick left by Will. *Dang Will, anyhow!* I tried not to make it obvious that I now had a furry grey hand, but Boss Ket was fighting back a smile.

I gave a small curtsy, then excused myself and walked away. A curtsy? I couldn't believe I curtsied! I was so shook at seeing Boss Ket, I almost walked right past Mr. Palmer. But I saw him out of the corner of my eye, turned around, and asked, "Excuse me, sir, are you Mr. Palmer?"

He looked at me and smiled politely. "Yes, I am," he said.

I smiled sweetly. "I've heard so much about you. My daddy says that you're helping everyone get stronger and more healthy. We're all so glad you're here."

Now he was really smiling. "Why, thank you."

"Sir, if you don't mind, I have a special present for you. A kitten."

He frowned and watched as I held up the basket for him to see, and pulled back the napkin, all the while maneuvering to keep my furry hand from showing. Eutychus, as if on command, sat up and yawned. Then he looked at Palmer and gave a little mew.

Mr. Palmer reached out and picked the kitten up, and Eutychus started his purring.

"What's his name?"

"We've called him Eutychus, but he's yours now,

so you can call him whatever you like."

"Eutychus, eh? How did he get that name?"

"Um, it's Biblical, but a long story. Believe me, he needs a safe loving home."

"Young lady, this is quite an unexpected surprise." He was quiet for several moments, then just as I was thinking he was going to say "No," he said, "Thank you so much. I had a cat at home in Europe that I had to leave behind, and I was missing him. This is really nice of you."

I couldn't believe it. I gave him the basket and made my getaway before Eutychus decided to throw himself in front of a carriage or get trampled by a mob of dancers. I fought the urge to run. I should have been sad to see him go, but I was so relieved that I'd passed him on in one piece I could hardly stand it. I stopped by where Will was working and gave him a big wave and then went to wait for my father.

When he pulled up, he asked, "Well, is Eutychus gone, did it work?"

"He's gone," I squealed and gave a little victory hop. Who would have expected that such a small kitten could bring so much joy?

CHAPTER TWENTY-FOUR

When I went into work the next week, I grabbed my broom and started sweeping. After about five minutes Boss Ket came in, gave me a big smile, and asked, "How'd you like that big party?"

"It was great!" I said. And then I stopped. Boss Ket's smile got bigger as my smile faded. *What had I done?* I wondered.

He stuck out his hand. "Name's Charles Kettering," he said, "but everyone calls me Boss Ket."

I stared at his hand for a moment, then I grabbed the broom with my left hand and shook his hand with my right hand.

"Leah Twist, but everyone calls me Lee. Glad to meet you, sir."

He threw his head back and laughed. "I knew it wouldn't be boring with you around. You're quite a gal, Lee."

Sunday I found out that I wouldn't be around for long. After church my parents called me into their bedroom and sat me down. "Lee, we know you're expecting to go back to school soon, but we need to ask you to do something."

I sat and waited, wondering what was going on. My mother swallowed, took a deep breath, and unfolded a piece of paper she was holding. "Honey, my little brother, Edwin, lives in Colorado. He's a good man and married a nice girl, Sarah. They have three young children and a new baby. Since Sarah gave birth, she's been having a rough time of it. Edwin wrote me and asked if we could send someone to help out. There's other family members living closer to him, but they all have their hands full. Your father and I both agree that you'd be the best one to go and stay for the winter, if you're willing—only if you're willing. You could attend school there."

Everything stopped. My brain, usually so busy, refused to move. I stared at my hands and fought back the tears.

"Do you want to think about this for a bit?" she asked. I nodded, and then stumbled out the door to my room.

Will was lurking in the hall, wondering what was up. I just shook my head and then ran to my room. It was awhile before I started thinking about anything. When I did, I almost wished I hadn't. Thoughts swirled around in my mind, as I wondered if I wasn't wanted, thinking my family might forget me, trying to figure out what I did wrong. Once those thoughts were exhausted, I sat some more. About that time, there was a soft knock at my door.

Mother opened it and came inside. She sat down beside me on the bed and wrapped her arms around me. She kissed me on the top of my head and said, "I love you, honey." And we sat. Finally she broke the silence. "Your father and I don't want you to go, you know. I'm going to miss you something terrible if you do go. But I have to be honest with you; they really need your help. Besides, I think you would love the adventure."

Adventure? I thought, *What adventure? I'd be taking care of kids—cooking, cleaning, sewing, laundry. That was not my idea of adventure. It was my idea of hell.*

She went on to explain. "They live up in the middle of the Rocky Mountains, close to where I grew up. It's like nothing you've ever seen or imagined. You'd take good care of them and still manage to have a great time. We'd send you out by train and your Uncle Edwin would meet you. If all goes well, you'll be back next spring, just in time to finish school with all your friends. And you'd miss fall harvesting."

"Wow, I have to go. No fall harvesting, neat."

We both laughed and she said, "Don't tell me now, just think about it and let me know. Then I'll send a note to Edwin and let him know if and when you'll be going. Since he works on a train, he'll send us a pass so that you can travel for free." She gave my shoulders another squeeze and left me alone.

I had to admit, once the shock was past, living in the Rocky Mountains did sound exciting. I hadn't heard much about my mother's brother. He was young when she left home. As I started thinking about it, I realized that I might get to meet my mother's whole family.

Living in Dayton, I was surrounded by Twists. Except for my Uncle David, I knew them all. Since my mother was from Colorado, we'd only heard bits and pieces about her family—she was the oldest and had three sisters and a little brother. She didn't talk much about growing up or Colorado. I think she missed them all so much she kept them inside her heart. I'd get to see where she came from.

I'd have to cook. That could be scary. I couldn't cook at all. They could all starve to death. I determined that I'd have to spend some time in the kitchen before I left.

With a start, I realized that I was already thinking in terms of going. Missing the family was going to be a big problem. But the adventure—and getting to help out, of course—proved to be too tempting to pass up. I was going to Colorado. In my tummy, the butterflies started to dance.

CHAPTER TWENTY-FIVE

I was going to Colorado. All of a sudden Will and Lin were extra nice to me, knowing that I'd be leaving in just a couple of weeks. I kept fighting back the urge to pinch myself to see if I was dreaming, but from all the packing I was doing, I knew it was for real. I also spent a bunch of time in the kitchen, desperately trying to soak up years of cooking know-how in a matter of days. The results of my efforts weren't encouraging, but my mother told me not to worry.

Will grabbed me one afternoon and told me I had to take one last trip out to Huffman Prairie. Lin was already out there. I was set on learning to cook, but Will kept after me. Finally, I decided it would be great to see the Wright brothers fly one more time before I left.

Once we got to the field, we found the airplane loaded up on the launch derrick, ready to go. The men, however, were inside.

Will and I walked over to the airplane to have a

closer look. I ran my hand along the wing and felt the tension on the wires. Will bent over and looked closely at the engine. The men were deep in conversation and hadn't noticed our arrival.

"Hey, Lee," Will said, "why don't you get on, see what it feels like."

"That's okay. *You* can, Will."

"Naw, you're leaving soon. This'll be special; I want you to."

I really wasn't sure that I wanted to, but Will was being so nice I couldn't say no. So I climbed up onto the airplane and stretched out like I'd seen the brothers do.

What a feeling. I was so excited as I laid down on the bottom wing, that I could hear my heart beating. There was this thing rigged up to steer by shifting your hips. I couldn't budge it, but I lay right in it.

Two handles were at the top edge of the wing where I lay. One, on the left, moved forward and back. Much to my delight, I realized that I could move it, and as I did that the elevators up front moved up and down. The other handle, on the right, moved from side to side. That one was harder to move. At first I didn't think it did anything, but then Will noticed that the back rudder moved when I moved the handle.

We stopped and listened. The men were talking about a letter they received. Wilber read part of it out loud. Sounded like the U.S. Army didn't want to invest in something that wasn't possible. I almost cried out, I was so mad. How could the U.S. Army be so wrong? We kept listening. Wilbur didn't sound happy; none of them did. At least we were okay to keep exploring. "You want to go next?" I asked. "This is great."

Before Will could answer, something terrible happened. The wing fabric was real smooth and I had been running my hand along it while listening to the men in the barn. Absentmindedly, I began fiddling with a metal clip underneath the wing. The clip sprang free. All of a sudden, the big weight began to drop and the plane started racing forward.

Will dropped to the ground just as the rudder passed over him. I grabbed on to the handle on the left, hoping that somehow it would stop the airplane, all the while screaming at the top of my lungs. The airplane didn't stop. It reached the end of the rail and left the ground with me still lying on the wing.

When it left the ground I stopped screaming. I was flying! It was really quiet because there was no engine running, and because there was no engine running, I didn't fly for long. I was only in the air for a few dozen yards, a few glorious moments. Then the plane bumped to the ground and stopped. I didn't move. I couldn't stop thinking about what had just happened. My mind was shouting, *I flew, I flew, I flew!* I was in the air, on a machine, and it went through the air, and I flew it. Well, I didn't *really* fly it, because I wasn't controlling it. If I had been controlling it, I would have stopped before ever getting off the ground . . . but I was glad I got off the ground because then I flew!

I took a deep breath and tried to calm down.

Behind me I could hear the men run up. One yelled, "Are you all right?" *Oh heck,* I thought, *I was in a load of trouble.* But it was worth it because that was the greatest thing in the whole world.

Once everyone reached me, they stood and stared. I looked up at them and smiled. When I finally caught my words, it was as if the heavens unleashed. "Oh, my gosh, did you see that? I was flying, I mean not like you, I don't know what I was doing, but I was in the air and in your plane and it was flying. It was wonderful. Thank you. And, oh, I'm so sorry, I didn't mean to, really. We were just looking and then I thought I'd just see how it felt to lay on the wing like you all and then the clip. You know, you really should rethink that clip, because I somehow did something to it because all of the sudden, well, you know, I was flying. And it was great!"

As I spoke, Charlie Taylor started to smile. He turned around, but I could hear him laughing. As I ran out of steam, Orville and Wilbur started to smile as well. Orville bent down close to my face and asked, "Are you all right?" I nodded. Then his eyes twinkled as he asked, "So, how'd you like it?"

"Mr. Wright, this here's the greatest invention in the whole wide world, and you two made it. You did what everyone thought couldn't be done. And riding on it was by far the most amazing thing I have ever done in my short lifetime. Yes, sir, I like it a whole bunch."

"Okay, then, you'd better help us get it back to the derrick."

"And then you can sweep up the barn," Wilber added.

I grabbed a hold of the plane and thought, *What is it with me and sweeping?*

CHAPTER TWENTY-SIX

It seemed like half a heartbeat later, I was on the platform waiting for the train. Lin, Will, Annie, and Jasper had said their goodbyes at home. I was glad we said goodbye there. We were quite a sight with the boys all nervous, Annie crying, and Jasper swiping his nose double-time. They even gave me a book, *Jo's Boys,* for the trip. As I got up into the buggy, Pork came over to say goodbye, and then to my surprise, Beans came and gave my hand a quick lick. That was the straw that broke the camel's back. I started to cry.

I quickly got up into the buggy and fussed with my shawl. I was wearing my Sunday best for the trip, which made the whole event even stranger. As the team pulled the buggy down the lane, I looked back at the house and waved at my brothers and sister. I tried to fix every face and every detail of our farm in my mind, knowing it would be a long while before I saw them again.

Once we got to the train station, my father left me to go check on the tickets. My mother went to fuss with the baggage. I looked around and saw, much to my surprise, Mr. Palmer. He had just gotten off a train. I looked frantically around for a place to hide, but I was standing in the middle of a train platform. There was nothing to hide behind. I turned away from him so that he wouldn't see me. I thought, *He probably doesn't even remember me.*

Then I heard a voice calling, "Young lady, excuse me. Young lady." Reluctantly I looked around. There stood Mr. Palmer.

It was too late to bolt. "Yes?" I asked, sweetly.

"Excuse me, but aren't you the girl that gave me that delightful kitten a few weeks ago?"

Delightful? I thought. "Why, yes sir, that was me."

He grabbed my hand and started to shake it enthusiastically, "I want to thank you for the kitten. He's made such a fine addition to my home. He's quite the pip. I just don't know what I did without him." With a final thank you, he turned around and walked away. I watched him go with my mouth gaping open.

My mother walked up beside me and watched him go. Then she asked, "Who was that?"

"That was Mr. Palmer," I explained. I told her what he had said. Just as I was finishing, my father walked up and my mother made me repeat the whole story to him.

They both laughed and gave me a big hug. "Oh, Lee," my father said, "It's going to be quiet around here without you."

"Yeah," my mother grinned, and gave me another big hug, "Don't you worry about the cooking. You'll be fine."

Just then the train whistle blew. It was time to get on board. In a flurry of activity, everything was loaded and last-minute instructions were given. I hugged both of them for a long while. The whistle blew again, and they both gave me a final kiss. They left the train, and I watched them as the train pulled out of the station.

I sat for a while thinking about my family and the summer I'd had. Then I took a deep breath and looked out the window, wondering what adventures Colorado held in promise.

GLOSSARY

People

Bill Chryst—He was Mr. Kettering's chief assistant. His conversation with Boss Ket about the Wright brothers really took place.

Edward Deeds—He was the man who hired Boss Ket, and rehired him as well (several times). They were great friends and later worked on several special projects together. Their first project was the automatic starter, which eliminated the need for a crank to start a car. The two friends developed many innovations that changed the way we live today.

Huffman Prairie Neighbor Lady—A real person, her name was Mrs. Beard. The Beards lived next door to Huffman Prairie, and Mrs. Beard kept an eye out for the Wright brothers. If she saw a rough landing or a crash, she was quick to run over and tend to their various cuts and bruises.

Mr. Jacobs—The knife sharpener, Mr. Jacobs, was not a real person, but the concept was accurate. Many vendors, including knife sharpeners, traveled from farm to farm selling their wares.

Charles Kettering—A remarkable man known by those who worked with him as Boss Ket. Although he looked mild-mannered, he was a real maverick. Mr. Kettering was a unique inventor for his day. Most inventors worked in secret, but he encouraged his men to work together and bounce ideas off each other. He began working at NCR in 1904, and was in charge of Inventions Department No. 3. The resulting "ordered chaos" in the department drove Mr. Patterson nuts. Consequently Boss Ket was fired on several occasions—and hired back again and again by Edward Deeds. One of his developments while at NCR was the electric cash register.

Years later, Mr. Kettering became known as the wizard of General Motors and is credited for having single-handedly set the American auto industry twenty-five years ahead of the rest of the world. Charles Kettering held 140 patents in his lifetime, second only to Thomas Edison.

Joe King and his Father—Fictional, but many people were fired because Mr. Palmer jumped to rash conclusions.

Charles Palmer—The story that was given about how he came to be the fitness guy at NCR is factual. He and Mr. Patterson did give a fitness demonstration, much to the amazement of all. His actions at NCR are based on fact (even down to what time of day he met with the executives). He never received a kitten that I know of, and I'm not sure his reaction would have been quite so kind—I just wanted to give the guy a break! It's gotta be rough being that disliked.

John H. Patterson—Although Mr. Patterson was not big physically, his presence was commanding. He was a man of unusual conviction. When he first started a factory that built cash registers, he was disappointed with the quality. Puzzled, he toured the factory. What he saw was typical for the time— dark, dirty, and dangerous, filled with unhappy people.

Patterson reasoned, "Why should they care about my product if I don't care about them?" He resolved to make a difference. He redesigned the factory: adding windows, cleaning the place up, and implementing safety practices. He worked at encouraging the employees by adding, among other things, a suggestion box, a lending library, and a fitness program. Employees were weighed, and if deemed too skinny, they were given malted milk. The grounds of the factory were just as unusual as the inside: beautifully landscaped. He proved to be a visionary—people were happy, and the quality of cash registers improved significantly. The factory became a model for factories around the country.

Mr. Patterson also changed the way traveling salesmen worked. Before this time traveling salesmen passed out cigars and smoozed the customers. Patterson taught his salesmen to inform the customer, act professional, and be the expert. And, yes, the chalk incident happened.

Mr. and Mrs. Stanley—The Gypsies were inspired by real events. Levi and Matilda Stanley, known as the king and queen of the Gypsies in the 1800's, owned land in Dayton, making the area a center for Gypsies. When Matilda died in 1878, more than 20,000 people from around the country, Canada, and England attended her funeral. Levi was still alive in 1905. The Stanley family was quite large. Each summer they would rent out their land to local farmers and travel around. Although there were rumors of Gypsies kidnapping babies and stealing horses, the Stanleys were churchgoing, respected members of the Dayton community.

Charlie Taylor—He worked for the Wright brothers for years and was instrumental in developing the engine for the early Wright Flyers.

Twist Family—Leo (father), Rose (mother), Lindley (Lin), Willard (Will), Leah (Lee), Anne and Jasper and extended family—fictional, but I borrowed the names from my aunts, uncles, grandparents, and father!

Wright Brothers—Both were very steady, kind men. Their physical descriptions and characters were based on fact. Wilber was 38 and Orville 34 years old the summer of 1905. Orville was a bit impish and Wilber was very serious. Both brothers were remarkable in their ability to think clearly, and their designs were achieved by painstaking research. Much of what is utilized in modern flight is still patterned after what they developed.

They were also known as the Bishop's boys because their father, Milton Wright, was a bishop in the United Brethren Church. He supported his sons and was present for their first flight at Huffman Prairie. They also had a sister, Katharine. Like their father, she was a great support to her brothers.

Places

Huffman Prairie—A local banker, Torrence Huffman, allowed the brothers to run their experiments in his field, located eight miles northeast of town. The Wright brothers built a small barn on the property. The description of the field is accurate, making learning how to fly (in every sense of the word) very interesting. Usually they stayed pretty close to the ground, so if they lost control they didn't have far to fall. The tree in the middle of the field was a honey locust, which is characterized by being covered with big thorns. I've seen one up close—ouch!

National Cash Register—NCR, The Register, The Cash— The descriptions throughout are very accurate, except for

146

where specific offices were located. Will's quotes were classic, 100% NCR. The factory was located on 131 acres, had nine main buildings, and five smaller buildings with a total of twenty-four acres of floor space, 140,000 panes of glass, and seventy-two janitors. There were 3,600 employees on the ledger that summer.

NCR's Inventions Department No. 3—Where Boss Ket worked. I endeavored to describe the office and the workers as accurately as possible. The tour by Mr. Patterson happened, resulting in Boss Ket being fired and the windows made so that no one could look in. I've read of two different ways that was accomplished; one account said that frosted glass was installed and another said that the glass was painted black so that no one could see in.

Summer Kitchen—Quite common at the time. A summer kitchen was built away from the main house and is where the cooking was primarily done during the summer (thus the name) to help keep the main house cooler during the hot days.

Spring Room—Part of the kitchen, or small closet just off the farmouse kitchen where spring water flowed and was captured in a large barrel. The family gathered their water from the barrel.

Things

Interurban—Part of the Ohio Electric Railway Company. It looked like a cross between a train and a trolley. At one time there were 600 miles of electric road in Ohio. It's popularity declined as more and more people purchased automobiles. It was a ten-minute ride (eight miles) from Dayton to Simms Station, and a train went by the station every thirty minutes. The platform sat across from the north end of the field with a line of trees between the two. The Wright brothers rode the interurban to Huffman field almost daily, at times toting tools or materials. Some people riding the interurban saw the Wright brothers flying; most paid no mind. Sometimes they called the local paper, asking about the goings-on at Huffman field, but the newspaper insisted that there was nothing to the flights and were quite put off by all the calls. Oops.

Launch Derrick—The size, development, and how the contraption worked is accurate. It was first used on September 7, 1904. Sometimes the Wright brothers positioned the plane on the derrick, ready to launch, and then went about other business. Sometimes it sat for hours before they flew.

Wright Flyer III—All the details about the airplanes are, to the best of my ability, accurate. Every day they flew they needed to assemble the Flyer first. At the end of the day they had to take it apart into three separate pieces. The barn they used was so small that the parts had to be fit inside like a puzzle. I'm not sure why they had skids instead of wheels—if you find out, let me know! The flyer was taken apart after the 1905 flying season. Forty-five years later it was put back together and is now on display at the Carillon Park Museum in Dayton, Ohio.

Animals

Beans—All made up. But I do have a dog with short red hair. Fortunately, her personality is more like Pork's.

Daisy—Fictional, but Morgan horses are a real breed of horses that began in the U.S. and are known for their sweet temperament and sturdiness.

Eutychus—Real! No kidding. He was our family cat, and I even toned down his story a bit.

Pork—All made up, but in 1905 a pig was a common pet. Theodore Roosevelt was the President of the United States at the time. His children had a pet pig. Many people thought it very improper to have a pig running around the White House, but others thought it was pretty cool. Pigs became the rage—quite the popular pet. Apparently they have great personalities.

Events

The Start of Flying Season—(Friday, June 23rd) When Lin, Will, and Lee first missed seeing the Wright brothers fly.
The Crash—(Friday, July 14th) It was just as described. It was really quite a miracle that Orville didn't get hurt. He was thrown through the wing and yet didn't hit a single wooden rib. The modifications to the elevator were made when they rebuilt the craft. The changes were key to the success of making the Wright Flyer III the first practical airplane.
NCR's Big Party—(Friday, July 21st) exactly as described in the 1905 NCR Newsletter, except I left out a few of the details; there wasn't enough room! There were 14,000 guests; 20,000 sandwiches; seventy barrels of lemonade; and 650 gallons of ice cream (among lots of other goodies) served. These folks knew how to throw a party!
NCR's Children's Ice Cream Party—(Friday, July 28th) Exactly as described, including the increase in numbers of children. Some 1,200 children were invited from vacation schools, and 2,000 showed up. Ten barrels of lemonade were gulped down, the children enjoyed Arabian and Egyptian tents and pictures from Mr. Patterson's trip, and then ice cream and cake was served. After all that was devoured, taffy and candy was handed out. Properly filled with sugar, they were sent home to their parents!

NCR's August Closing—(August 1st–12th) Yes, the first two weeks of August the factory closed. (There was no air conditioning and working conditions were miserable: not a lot of work got done during that time.) There was a big NCR outing to the Great Lakes during that time.

First Flight After Modifications—(August 24th) The plane was just as successful as described. It was a turning point for the brothers.

Cotillion—This was the one event that didn't happen on the day I have it in the book! It actually took place earlier that summer (June 8th), but I needed a time where the kids could buttonhole Mr. Palmer. The event was described in the NCR Newsletter as 600 men and women dancing and performing various pieces. The women wore white dresses and colorful scarves; a variety of hats and other objects were added for different dances. It was all quite pretty. There were 500 additional guests, and after the dancing was performed, there was a picnic and dancing.

Extras

The Bee Keeper—"Gleanings in Bee Culture," Volume XXXIII, January 15, 1905, Number 2, by Amos I. Root, from Medina, Ohio—For quite awhile, it was the only paper that contained an account of the Wright brothers flying.

NCR's Executive Riding Program—There was such a thing, and yes, people did get hurt, including Charles Kettering.

The Wright Brother's Letter from the Army—The Wright brothers kept writing the Army, letting them know about their airplane, and they kept getting brushed off. No one took them seriously for three more years. Although frustrated, the Wright brothers never gave up.